Geronimo Stilton

THE SHIP OF SECRETS

THE TENTH ADVENTURE IN THE KINGDOM OF FANTASY

Scholastic Inc.

Published by Scholastic Inc., *Publishers since 1920*, 557 Broadway, New York, NY 10012. SCHOLASTIC and associated logos are trademarks and/or registered trademarks of Scholastic Inc.

Stilton is the name of a famous English cheese. It is a registered trademark of the Stilton Cheese Makers' Association. For more information, go to www.stiltoncheese.com.

This book is a work of fiction. Names, characters, places, and incidents are either the product of the author's imagination or are used fictitiously, and any resemblance to actual persons, living or dead, business establishments, events, or locales is entirely coincidental.

Library of Congress Cataloging-in-Publication Data available

ISBN 978-1-338-08880-9

Text by Geronimo Stilton
Original title *Decimo Viaggio nel Regno della Fantasia*
Cover by Silvia Bigolin (design) and Christian Aliprandi (color)
Illustrations by Silvia Bigolin, Carla De Bernardi, Alessandro Muscillo, Federico Brusco, and Piemme's Archives. Color by Christian Aliprandi.
Graphics by Marta Lorini

Special thanks to AnnMarie Anderson
Translated by Andrea Schaffer
Interior design by Kay Petronio

10 9 8 7 6 5 4 3 2 1   17 18 19 20 21

Printed in China   38

First edition, July 2017

Protectors
of the Kingdom of Fantasy

Geronimo Stilton

I am a bestselling author, and I run *The Rodent's Gazette*, the most famouse newspaper on Mouse Island. I often travel to the Kingdom of Fantasy to help Queen Blossom. This is my tenth visit!

Scribblehopper

I am Geronimo's guide on his visits to the Kingdom of Fantasy. I am a chatty frog with a big heart. I dream of writing a bestselling book someday!

Blossom

I am known as the Queen of the Fairies, the White Queen, and the Lady of Peace and Happiness. I hope to unite the world in love, light, and harmony.

Sweet Melinda

I am the Princess of the Vanilla Fairies, the only fairies in the Kingdom of Fantasy that look like young mice with wings! I am Queen Blossom's dear friend.

The Dragonfly Princesses

We reign over the giant dragonflies that live in Sweetwater Lake, next to Crystal Castle.

Wink

I am the fastest of the Blue Weasels. I am curious, generous, and ready to do whatever it takes to save the Blue Weasels!

THE BEST COUSIN
IN THE WORLD…

It was a gloomy Friday afternoon in New Mouse City. The weather was **DAMP** and **cold**, and I was holed up in my office, hard at work.

Oops, I'm sorry! I haven't introduced myself yet. My name is Stilton, *Geronimo Stilton*! I run *The Rodent's Gazette*, the most **FAMOUSE** **newspaper** on Mouse Island.

Anyway, as I was saying, I was in the office and a **thunderstorm** was brewing. The wind was *blowing* so hard it rattled the windows and bent the branches of the trees. For a second, I thought I heard a strange voice outside:

"Kniiiight! Kniiiight! Kniiiight! Kniiiight! Kniiiight! Kniiiight! Kniiiight! Kniiiight!"

I ran to look out the window, but all I saw were rodents SCURRYING to get indoors. **How strange!** It was probably all in my imagination. Or it could have been just the sound of the *WIND*...

I worked until the late afternoon, while the sky grew darker and more threatening. In the distance, I heard the booming of thunder. Then suddenly, the door to my office flew open!

Someone dressed in a BLACK jacket, a fluttering **red silk** cape, and a top hat

came in. He was holding a cane with a **skull-shaped** knob at the end. He wore a black **M A S K** over his snout, and in his right paw, he carried a small crystal bottle full of a sparkling red liquid. Behind him, he pulled a red, velvet-lined COFFIN on wheels. But the most **TERRIFYING** thing about this mysterious rodent was that he had fangs just like a vampire!

"*Aaaaaahhhh!*" I screamed.

I turned as pale as mozzarella. I'm not brave at all . . . In fact, I'm a real scaredy-mouse!

Then a bolt of lightning LIT UP the room. ZING!

A second later, the lights went out!

Before I fainted from fright, the mysterious mouse giggled.

"Geronimo, you really are easy to fool," the mouse said.

It was only then that I recognized his voice. I looked more closely and saw that the TEETH were made of plastic. Furthermore, the mouse's paw was on the light switch. The lights hadn't gone out — he had FLICKED them off!

"You're not a vampire," I said accusingly. "You're my cousin **TRAP**!"

"Oh, Gerrykins, you're so gullible!" he said, laughing. "So, what do you think of my **vampire**

Who was the vampire who had come into my office?

It was my cousin Trap! His teeth were fake and the bottle was filled with tomato juice!

costume? I figured I'd try it out on you to see how **authentic** it is."

I dried the sweat from my forehead. My whiskers were still **trembling** with fear.

"Ha, ha," I said weakly. "It's a very **GOOD** costume. But you almost scared me **OUT OF MY FUR**!"

"Oh, come on, Gerry Berry." He snickered. "Can't you take a little joke? I'm the **best** cousin in the world, right?"

"Well, you aren't boring," I replied. My cousin can be a bit **MUCH**.

"I just **knew** you'd like my costume," Trap continued, smiling proudly. "Now aren't you going to ask **WHY** I'm dressed like a vampire, **Germeister**?"

"No, thanks!" I said. "I'm really not interested, Trap. I'm very busy **WORKING**. And my name is Geronimo. That's **G-E-R-O-N-I-M-O**!"

Trap drank a sip of **tomato juice**, cleaned his whiskers on my tie, and giggled.

"But I think you'll find it **very** interesting, Geronimo," he said slyly. "After all, you're invited, too!"

He **WAVED** a card under my nose, but I couldn't see what it said.

Then Trap read aloud: "'Mr. Geronimo Stilton is invited to the *New Mouse City Grand Masked Ball*. All guests must arrive dressed

Mr. Geronimo Stilton is invited to the New Mouse City Grand Masked Ball. All guests must arrive dressed as their favorite fantasy characters. Costumes are mandatory — no exceptions! The ball begins Friday at midnight in the ballroom at Goldenfur Castle.

as their favorite fantasy characters. Costumes are mandatory — **NO EXCEPTIONS**! The ball begins Friday at midnight in the ballroom at Goldenfur Castle.'"

On the back of the invite there was a note: "'By the way, don't be late! There will be an all-you-can-eat **CHEESE BUFFET**, but it's first come, first served!'"

MASKS FOR MICE

I hit my head with my paw. The Grand Masked Ball was the most famous party in New Mouse City, and it was happening **tonight**! I had completely forgotten.

"Chewy cheddar chunks!" I squeaked. "I promised Creepella von Cacklefur I would go with her, but I don't have a costume yet."

Trap just shook his head.

"Oh, Gerry Berry, you're in **TROUBLE**," he said in a singsong voice. "Creepella has a **TERRIBLE TEMPER**!"

I absolutely had to fix this. So I called my sister, Thea, RIGHT AWAY.

"Hi, Thea," I said quickly. "Where can I find a **COSTUME** for tonight's masked ball?"

"Are you **kidding**?" came her reply. "Everyone knows the stores in New Mouse City don't have any costumes left!"

I was about to cry.

Creepella might be my friend, but she has a **TERRIBLE TEMPER**! I told her I would go to the ball with her months ago! What in the

Oh no!

Oh, help!

What a disaster!

1 I had forgotten that the Grand Masked Ball was tonight!

2 I didn't have a costume yet . . .

3 And my date — my friend Creepella — has a terrible temper!

name of **CHEESE** was I going to do?

But then Thea had an **IDEA**.

"Wait a minute, Geronimo!" she squeaked. "You could try my friend Felicia Fashionfur's store. It's called **Masks for Mice**, and it's at thirteen Masquerade Lane. Give her my name, okay? Hopefully she can help you."

I dashed out the door right away and flagged down a **TAXI**.

"Number thirteen Masquerade Lane," I told the driver. "And please *hurry*!"

A few minutes later, the taxi stopped in front of a store with a large painted **WOODEN** sign that read **Masks for Mice**. This was it!

As I paid my driver, I noticed that a mouse dressed as a **WITCH** was locking up the shop.

"Wait!" I squeaked. "Please don't close! I need a costume **right away**!"

The rodent at the door was wearing a **pointy**

hat, a **PURPLE** silk dress, and pointy-toed **shoes**.

"You're Thea's brother, Geronimo, right?" she asked.

"Um, yes, that's me," I replied. "My name is Stilton, *Geronimo Stilton*, and I need —"

She cut me off before I could finish.

"I know what you need," she said. "A **costume** for tonight's ball! But I don't have any left. That's how it goes — it's the **BEST** party of the year! Everyone's going, even me! I'm dressed as a **witch**. What do you think of my costume?"

"It's **great**," I replied. Then I fell to my knees, **SOBBING**. "But don't you have a costume for me, too? Any costume will do — I'll take **whatever you've got**! Otherwise Creepella will —"

Felicia **shuddered** and then interrupted me again.

"**Moldy mozzarella!**" she exclaimed. "Say no more. I went to school with Creepella. She's a great friend, but that mouse has a **TERRIBLE TEMPER**! Follow me inside and let's see what I can find."

I followed her up a **spiral** staircase and into a **D A R K** room. I was feeling hopeful, until my eyes adjusted to the dark. All around me

I'll take anything!

Creepella?

were thousands and thousands and thousands of hangers — but they were all EMPTY!

Felicia began to rummage around in a corner.

"Oh, it must be here . . . or maybe here . . . or it could be there," she muttered. "Oh, here it is! I knew I'd find it SOMEWHERE!"

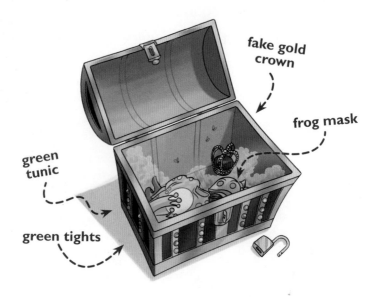

fake gold crown

frog mask

green tunic

green tights

Finally, at the bottom of a very dusty trunk, she found a **GREEN** tunic and tights, a **FROG** mask, and a fake gold **CROWN** decorated with fake stones. There was also a broken chain with a **MEDALLION** on it that read:

WHO WANTS TO KISS ME?

JUST LIKE A FROG . . .

"B-but what's this?" I asked.

"Why, it's a **FROG PRINCE** costume!" Felicia replied brightly. "It's perfect for tonight's ball. The theme is fantasy characters, you know!"

I put on the **costume** and placed the medallion around my neck and the crown on my head. Then we went into the store. Felicia pushed me in front of a giant **mirror**.

"When you wear this costume, you must **stay in character!**" she explained. "That means you have to:

- stay crouched, like a **FROG** . . .
- keep your knees bent, like a **FROG** . . .
- move by jumping, like a **FROG** . . .
- talk by croaking, just like a **FROG**!

"The crown on your head shows that you are waiting for a *beautiful princess* to kiss you," she continued. "Then you'll turn into a prince. **Watch out**, Geronimo! Who knows how many rodents will try to **SMOOCH** you tonight!"

She giggled.

"So, what do you say?" Felicia asked. "Do you **like** it? Do you **WANT** it? Are you taking the costume or not? I need to close the shop and go home to finish **GETTING READY**. I'm going to the party, too, remember?"

I didn't know what to say. I really didn't want to dress like a **FROG**, and I certainly didn't want

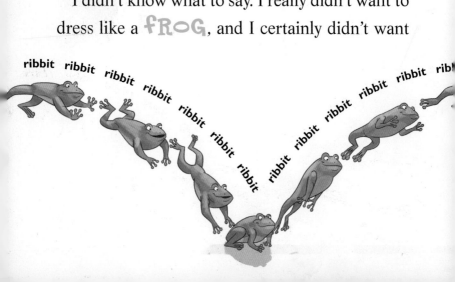

ribbit ribbit ribbit ribbit ribbit ribbit ribbit ribbit ribbit ribbit rib

every rodent at the ball trying to **kiss me**!

"Er, thanks, Felicia," I replied. "This costume is, um, nice, but it's really **SILLY**! I'm a very *serious* mouse! I run *The Rodent's Gazette*, and I need a *serious* costume. Something like a KNIGHT or a **wizard** or a **KING**. I'd be too embarrassed to go to the ball as a fROG PRINCe!"

Felicia just shrugged.

"Suit yourself," she said **simply**. "If you don't want it, that's okay. BYE!"

She headed toward the door, but I stopped her.

"WAIT!" I squeaked. "Please help me, Felicia!"

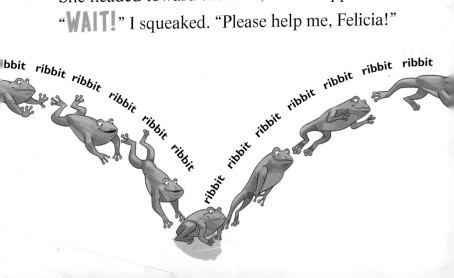

ribbit ribbit ribbit ribbit ribbit ribbit ribbit ribbit ribbit ribbit ribbit ribbit

She just sighed.

"What can I do, Geronimo?" she said. "Until this morning, I had a lot of **beautiful** costumes. There were **RED**, **YELLOW**, and **GREEN DRAGONS** (with or without wings); wizards and sorcerers; kings (with or without crowns); knights, complete with white horses; gnomes; goblins; trolls; and some truly **nightmarish** characters. I had monsters without heads, ghosts in chains, and vampires, too! Your cousin Trap rented a *fang*tastic **vampire** costume."

My eyes filled with tears again at the thought of all the **WONDERFUL** costumes I had missed.

"I know," I said sadly. "I made an **enormouse** mistake. But what do I do now?"

She put her paw on my shoulder.

"Just give it a chance, Geronimo," she said. "Wear the frog prince costume. It's better than **nothing**, right?"

I sighed. "You're right," I said. "Now, how much is this going to **cost me**?"

"I'll give it to you as a **gift**," she said with a smile. "Your sister is my *friend*, after all. And no one else is still looking for a costume at this hour anyway!"

I thanked her for her **generosity** and headed home.

How **silly** of me to forget the date of the ball! It was my own fault that I had to dress like the **FROG PRINCE**. It was evening now, and the streets were emptying. Everyone in New Mouse City was **CHEERFULLY** getting ready for the *Grand Masked Ball*!

It seemed like I was the only one feeling **down in the snout.**

Sigh . . .

Here are all the costumes

Knight

Wizard

King

Jester

Vampire

Santa Claus

Dragon

Robin Hood

Gnome

I could have worn . . .

Frankenstein

Dr. Jekyll

Witch

Elf

Ogre

Ghost

Pirate

And here's
the one
I got!

Frog Prince

Goldenfur Castle

As soon as I got home, I put on the costume. It was even more **UNCOMFORTABLE** than it had been in the store! I crouched down and practiced my jumping, but my legs CRAMPED. I shined the gold chain and medallion to make them more sparkly before I put the necklace around my neck. Finally, I placed the crown with the fake jewels on top of my head.

I sighed. It was too late to find another costume, so I had to make the **BeSt** of this one!

I went outside and hailed the first T A X I that came by. But when the driver saw me, he burst out laughing!

"Ha, ha, ha," he chuckled. "I've never had a frog passenger before! I hope you don't pay me with **flies**!"

My Frog Prince Costume

Profile view

The front

Three-quarter turn

While I try to jump

While I perfect my jump

Practically flying

A perfect frog!

He was just JOKING around, but I was too down in the snout to **laugh**.

"Please take me to . . ." I muttered.

But he finished the sentence for me.

"To **GOLDENFUR CASTLE**, of course!" he said. "You're going to the Grand Masked Ball, right? Where else would a **FROG PRINCE** be going on a Friday night? Ha, ha, ha!"

We took the road along the waterfront, and I again thought I heard a strange voice:

"Kniiiight! Kniiiight! Kniiiight! Kniiiight! Kniiiight! Kniiiight! Kniiiight! Kniiiight!"

I looked out the window but didn't see anyone. **How strange!** Maybe it was just my imagination, or the sound of the wind, or the waves crashing against the shore. **WHO KNOWS!**

The taxi stopped at the top of a **HILL** just

The Story of the Grand Masked Ball

The Grand Masked Ball was conceived of in 1654 by **Princess Whiskerella Goldenfur**. It takes place each year on her birthday, and it is held in Goldenfur Castle's grand ballroom. The castle is famouse for its sparkling golden roof and its fairy-tale-like décor. The princess wanted everyone to experience the castle's legendary beauty, so the ball was open to all the

Princess Whiskerella Goldenfur

citizens of New Mouse City. Whiskerella was passionate about fairy tales, so she wanted everyone at the **Grand Masked Ball** to dress like characters from her favorite stories. Each year, all of the rodents in New Mouse City compete to show off the most original costume. The winner is named the "King of Fantasy" or the "Queen of Fantasy." They get to wear a pure-gold crown for a year, until the next king or queen is crowned.

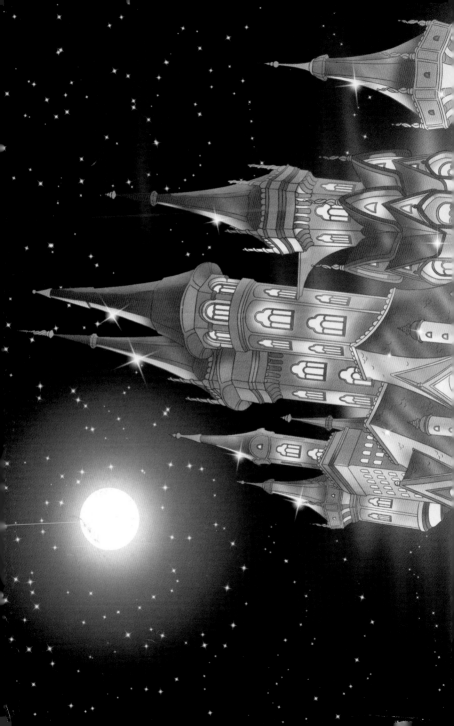

before we reached the castle. The headlights illuminated the building, which was lit by thousands of **sparkling** lights.

"Here we are," the taxi driver said as he dropped me off. "Have a good night! I hope you get that special **kiss** so you can change out of that **silly** frog costume. Ha, ha, ha!"

With a resigned sigh, I headed into the castle and joined the crowd of **COSTUMED** rodents. I found myself in the **magnificent** ballroom.

Oh, Goldenfur Castle was so beautiful!

The room was lit by **CRYSTAL** chandeliers and the tables were covered in fine linen tablecloths and laden with **delicious dishes**: cheesecakes, mountains of fresh mozzarella, Swiss fondue, cheddar milkshakes, and chocolates filled with Gorgonzola. **YUM!**

The guests' **COSTUMES** were fantastic!

There were fairies and wizards, princes and princesses, kings and queens, and knights and ladies. There were also *winged* dragons, SPOOKY ghosts, and **scary** witches! Of course I was the only one there in a **RIDICULOUS** frog prince costume. Embarrassed, I slipped out of the ballroom into the garden, where I hid behind a **marble fountain** to watch the festivities.

The water in the fountain trickled with a soft, *pleasant* sound. For a second, I thought I heard a strange voice in the night:

"Kniiiight! Kniiiight! Kniiiight! Kniiiight! Kniiiight! Kniiiight! Kniiiight! Kniiiight! Kniiiight!"

I looked around, but I didn't see anyone near me dressed like a knight. How strange! It might have been the sound of the water. Or maybe it was just my *IMAGINATION* . . .

No Kisses, Please!

After I had been hiding in the garden for about fifteen minutes, my stomach began to **GROWL**. I thought about the delectable foods I had seen on the cheese buffet table. I just had to have one of those **Gorgonzola tarts**! I checked to be sure my mask fit snugly over my snout and then I headed back inside. As I jumped toward the snacks, I heard **squeaks** behind me.

How funny!

Stunning!

What a costume!

He's a brave mouse!

"What an original costume!"

"That mouse is really staying in **character**!"

"How silly!"

"He must be brave to wear a costume like that!"

"Look at his medallion! It reads **'Who wants to kiss me?'**!"

A female rodent stepped forward.

"I'll try!" she squeaked. "Let's see if this **fROG** turns into a **PRINCE**!"

At that moment, a **SHADOW** fell across the marble floor. A mouse dressed in purple

Help!

Oh no you don't!

SWUNG her purse at the **unfortunate** mouse who had tried to kiss me.

"Oh no you don't!" she squeaked. "This frog is ***all mine***!"

YIKES! It was my date, Creepella von Cacklefur! In addition to having a **TERRIBLE TEMPER**, Creepella can be a bit, well, jealous! Even though I was the one dressed in green, it seemed Creepella was green with envy!

"It's about time you arrived!" Creepella scolded me. "You're late! But I'll **forgive** you."

Then she leaned over and tried to give me a huge **smooch** on the snout.

Somehow I managed to **DODGE** her.

"Um, no, thanks, Creepella," I mumbled. "I'm not really in the MOOD for kisses tonight!"

38

Creepella put her paws on her hips.

"Well, why are you wearing that SIGN around your neck then, huh?" she asked.

As if I wasn't **embarrassed** enough, mice all around us began WHISPERING.

"Who's that mouse with Creepella?" someone said. "Some date! He won't even KISS her!"

"I think it's *Geronimo Stilton*!" another mouse replied.

"You mean the famouse **newspaper** mouse?" another gasped.

"Hey, frog prince," another mouse squeaked. "Show your snout!"

Come here!

No, thanks!

I was so embarrassed I wanted to **MELT** into the floor like mozzarella on a pizza. I didn't know what else to do, so I took off my **mask**.

"It **is** him!" a mouse squeaked in shock. "What a **rude** rodent!"

Creepella squinted at me.

"Yeah, what a **rude** date you are, Geronimo!" she agreed. Then she **SWUNG** her purse at me! Unfortunately, the froggy feet on my costume weren't very **STEADY**, and I lost my balance as I dodged her bag. I **wobbled** on my paws, and a second later, I landed in the ballroom's famous **WATER LILY FOUNTAIN**.

SPLASH!

I must have **BUMPED** my head when I fell into the fountain, because I saw so many stars I felt like I was in **outer space**!

I fell deeper and deeper into the water.

When I came to, I realized I was no longer at **GOLDENFUR CASTLE** on Mouse Island. Instead, I was in a beautiful, magical place I had been many times before . . . the *Kingdom of Fantasy*!

The Kingdom
of Fantasy

SWEET MELINDA

I knew I wasn't in New Mouse City anymore because the mouse standing in front of me when I opened my eyes wasn't Creepella. This tiny, mysterious rodent wore the gold crown of a princess. She also had small, transparent fairy wings on her back, just like Blossom, the Queen of the Fairies!

Wake up, Knight!

Her snout was very delicate: Her little nose seemed like a rosebud; her eyes were the color of periwinkles, and her whiskers looked to be as soft as silk. Her shimmery dress was a lovely light blue that matched her eyes PERFECTLY. But the thing that struck me most about her was the sweet smell of vanilla that hung in the air all around her!

"Sir Knight!" she whispered sweetly. "Please wake up!"

I rubbed the top of my head. It still hurt where I had bonked it in the fountain.

"Er, yes, I'm awake," I replied. "Who am I? Um, I mean, where am I, and who are you?"

"I am Sweet Melinda," she said SOFTLY, placing her little paw over her heart. "I'm the Princess of the Vanilla Fairies. You are Sir Geronimo of Stilton, and this is the Kingdom of Fantasy! This is the Enchanted Lagoon behind us.

Isn't it beautiful?"

"Princess of the Vanilla Fairies?" I asked, confused. Who were they? I had never met any mouse fairies on my other visits to the Kingdom of Fantasy. And I had never been to the Enchanted Lagoon, either!

I stood up and looked around. In front of me was a calm, CLEAR blue sea. Behind me was a forest of coconut trees. And there was a SOFT, sandy beach under my paws. It seemed like PARADISE!

For a moment, I took it all in. Then I looked above me. A majestic black ship seemed to be sailing through the starry night sky, leaving a trail of moon dust behind it!

I stared at it with my mouth open: I had never seen such an extraordinary sight!

Suddenly, there was a large FLASH of light. The ship DOVE straight toward the ground, landing

in a grove of palm trees nearby.

The princess gasped.

"Let's go, Knight!" she squeaked. "They're here!"

"Huh?" I exclaimed as she pulled me by the paw.

"Who's HERE?"

"Shhh!" she whispered softly as we hid behind some bushes. "It's a long story. For now, you just need to know that they're **WICKED** and **DANGEROUS** . . . and there are a lot of them!

"Look! It's **Captain Shorttail** and the Ship of Secrets!"

In the distance, I heard voices singing a **SUPER-SCARY** song:

AHOY THERE, PIRATES, BOLD AND TRUE,

WHO'S THE FIERCEST RAT IN THE PIRATE CREW?

YO, HO, HO! CAPTAIN SHORTTAIL'S HIS NAME.

YO, HO, HO! BEING MEAN IS HIS GAME.

HE HAS A BLOODRED BEARD AND A LONG FUR-DO,

AND A SWORD SO SHARP IT'LL SLICE YOU IN TWO!

YO, HO, HO! CAPTAIN SHORTTAIL'S HIS NAME.

YO, HO, HO! BEING MEAN IS HIS GAME.

HE'LL MAKE YOU WALK THE PLANK JUST FOR FUN,

IF YOU SEE HIM COMING, YOU'D BETTER RUN!

YO, HO, HO! CAPTAIN SHORTTAIL'S HIS NAME.

YO, HO, HO! BEING MEAN IS HIS GAME.

How Bad Is He?

Once we were hidden, Melinda told me her story.

"Knight, please let me explain who I am and why you are here in the *Kingdom of Fantasy*," she began.

"I probably already know!" I interrupted her. "I imagine Queen Blossom has a MISSION for me and that she sent you here with a message that explains everything . . ."

She shook her head, tears shining in her blue eyes.

"No, Knight," she said softly. "I'm the one who CALLED YOU! Now if you have the patience to listen to my story, I'll explain everything."

As Melinda squeaked, the sweet scent of vanilla filled the air all around us. It was ENCHANTING!

Sweet Melinda
Princess of the
Vanilla Fairies

The Story of Sweet Melinda and

I am **Sweet Melinda**, the Princess of the **Vanilla Fairies**. We are the only fairies in the Kingdom of Fantasy who look like mice, but with wings! I am one of Blossom's dear friends. My kingdom is small but fragrant because it is covered with **magic flowers**. The Vanilla Fairies extract a **special** golden pollen from these flowers. We then turn it into a **magic** powder called vanilla dust!

Vanilla dust is a specialty on the **Vanilla Islands**: just a small pinch and anything will be able to fly, from a **tiny** mouse to an **enormouse** ship! The Vanilla Fairies store the dust in a precious silver coffer to keep it safe.

the Vanilla Islands' Magic Flowers

Unfortunately, one **dark** night when there was no **moon**, a group of ferocious pirates landed their **nightmarish** ship here. The pirates stole the coffer of vanilla dust and kidnapped me!

The pirates used the vanilla dust to make the *Ship of Secrets* **fly**. I was able to escape, but I live in fear that the pirates' ferocious leader, Captain Shorttail, will find me. I also know the captain's secret: He is an ally of the biggest, most **powerful** and **dangerous** wizard in the Kingdom of Fantasy — the **Whopping Wizard**! Captain Shorttail even gave him all of the **vanilla dust**!

Hee, hee, hee!

Let me go!

When Melinda finished her story, I didn't know what to say: Those pirates sounded really **cruel** and **evil**!

"Now do you understand why I called you here?" she asked. "I am in **grave** danger! But I know you can help me, **BRAVE** knight. You've saved my friend Blossom many times, and she told me that you are very **courageous** and not

afraid of anything. She said you even know how to **defeat** dragons, witches, and giants!"

"Ahem, well, I guess I have done those things before," I muttered. "And I have been courageous sometimes. But this **Captain Shorttail** sounds very ferocious. Tell me: **How bad is he?**"

She looked at me in surprise.

"Why, Sir Geronimo, your whiskers are **trembling**!" she exclaimed. "And your teeth

are chattering! Why are you so **PALE**? You're a brave knight! Are you afraid of Captain Shorttail and his band of **terrible** pirates?"

I was too embarrassed to admit that **YES**, I, Sir Geronimo of Stilton, was **afraid**. So I made up an excuse.

"Er, well, you know, the seawater was so **cold**, I think I caught a little chill!" I replied, shivering.

"Honestly, I wouldn't blame you for being **scared**," Melinda said sweetly. "Captain Shorttail is really, really **FEROCIOUS**! Everyone in the Kingdom of Fantasy is afraid of him! Let me tell you **why** . . ."

THE TERRIFYING STORY OF CAPTAIN SHORTTAIL

Captain Shorttail descends from an ancient family of terrifying pirates, the Pirates of the Ship of Secrets. His first name is Sammy, but he was given the nickname Shorttail because a shark devoured half of his tail when he was just a tiny rat! Shorttail is a real pirate: He's a lazy, dishonest, greedy liar who is willing to do whatever it takes to become rich, rich, rich! When he's not out sailing the seas, he's in his secret hideout. But no one knows where that is! It is rumored that Captain Shorttail has hidden thirteen trunks of silver treasure in this mysterious place.

ALL THE PIRATES IN CAPTAIN SHORTTAIL'S FAMILY ARE SUPER-SCARY!

Captain Shorttail is the son of the celebrated pirate Whiskerless Willy. He got that nickname when his enemy cut off all his whiskers during battle and they never grew back. Whiskerless Willy married the legendary pirate Sabrina Saberpaw, who was named because of her amazing ability to duel with a saber.

The two had only one son, Sammy Shorttail.

SAMMY SHORTTAIL

As soon as Melinda finished speaking, the bushes around us **rustled**. A moment later, I saw the **LIGHT** of approaching lanterns and smelled the **stinky stench** of someone who hadn't bathed in a long, long, long time . . .

What a stink!

Come on!

"Come on!" Melinda whispered urgently. "Let's get out of here!"

But it was too late. A second later, the light of an oil lamp fell on my snout.

A deep voice grumbled loudly . . .

"WELL, LOOKY HERE! I FOUND A STRANGE LITTLE CASTAWAY!"

I was facing a short, stocky rat with a bumpy nose, a FIERCE glare, one crooked tooth, and a chopped-off tail!

It was

Captain Sammy Shorttail!

"Come CLOSER, castaway," he growled. "I want to get a better look at you . . ."

He held the oil lamp up to my snout and GLARED at me.

"Hmmm." He sneered. "Are you a **mouse** or a fROG? I really can't tell! All I know is, you're definitely **NOT** who I was looking for!"

Then he raised the lantern and illuminated Melinda's snout.

"She's the one I'm after!" he shouted, grinning triumphantly.

He smoothed his whiskers, a satisfied look on his snout.

"What an excellent **SURPRISE** this

is! Welcome back to the pirate crew, Princess Melinda. You thought you could escape, but **NO ONE** escapes from Captain Shorttail!"

"Wait!" I cried, trying my best to be ***brave***. "Let the princess go! Take **ME** as your prisoner instead!"

"Ha, ha, ha!" Captain Shorttail cackled evilly. "Listen to this f𝖱O𝖦 — I mean, **mouse**! He thinks I'm going to let one of them 𝖌𝖔! Who is he kidding? Ha, ha, ha!"

Suddenly, a voice behind him called out: "Yoo-hoo! Captain Shorttail! When are you going to get me that deckhand/dishwasher/potato peeler/ ship cleaner/toilet washer I asked for?"

A New Deckhand
for Chef Greasypaw

The rodent who had yelled at Captain Shorttail emerged from the bushes. He was a **plump** rat with **greasy** black whiskers, small beady eyes that looked like black olives, and enormouse ears that looked like two heads of cauliflower. He wore a cook's apron dotted with SPOTS of grease, butter, chocolate, and cheese sauce. On his head was a tall cook's hat with a GREEN PARROT perched on top.

As the cook approached us, I noticed that he was stirring a pot of a foul-smelling soup with a large metal spoon.

"Ah, it's Chef Greasypaw!" Captain Shorttail said gleefully. "Greasy, today is your lucky day: Here is your new **DECKHAND**! Or should I say deckmouse? Or maybe deckfrog? I have **NO IDEA**! Ha, ha, ha!"

"Excellent!" Chef Greasypaw cried. "I'll call you FLYCATCHER, because you're a frog who eats flies! Also, it will be part of your job to catch extra flies to add to my **YUMMY** soups! Get it? Ha, ha, ha!"

"Sir Knight," Melinda whispered to me. "Do you have a plan to SAVE us?"

Chef Greasypaw
He is the cook aboard the *Ship of Secrets*. He prepares slop so gross only Captain Shorttail and his crew are able to eat it! The minestrone of rotten cabbage is his signature dish: To make it more delicious, he flavors it with flies, spiders, and cockroaches that he finds on board the ship. He never goes anywhere without his pet parrot, Salty!

"Uh, I'm working on it!" I replied. I had to come up with something *FAST*! But how could we escape from these **AWFUL** pirates?

Chef Greasypaw began pushing me forward, prodding me in the tail with a large metal fork.

"Hurry up, Flycatcher!" he ordered. "There's plenty of **WORK** waiting for you at the ship!"

"Okay!" I squeaked, rubbing my tail. "I'm going. You don't need to **POKE** me!"

Flycatcher!

Ouch!

What's the plan?

But he continued to pinch, poke, and prod my tail as we walked down a stony trail that led to a small HIDDEN lagoon.

An enormouse black ship was anchored there, the name **Ship of Secrets** painted on its side! It was completely BLACK, from its hull to its sails. Terrifying pirate flags waved from each mast.

A tremendous stench emanated from the ship. It stank . . .

. . . worse than a troll's ARMPITS!

. . . worse than a witch's breath!

. . . worse than an ogre's FEET!

Ugh, what an offensive odor!

The Ship of Secrets is anchored in a hidden lagoon!

THE SECRETS OF THE *SHIP OF SECRETS*

Chef Greasypaw quickly showed me around the ship. Then he led me to the kitchen and made me change into pirate deckhand's **clothes**: a red bandanna, a *frilly* white shirt, a pair of **GREEN** pants, and a **LEATHER** belt with a gold buckle.

Then he gave me a **scrub brush**.

Geronimo dressed as the frog prince

Geronimo dressed as Flycatcher the deckhand

BEFORE

AFTER

"Flycatcher, have you seen how big the *Ship of Secrets* is? Have you seen how **LONG** the deck is? Have you seen how **greasy** the kitchen is? Have you seen how many **dirty** plates are in the sink? And have you seen how many **potatoes** are in that sack? You will clean **EVERYTHING** on the ship! You will polish the **ENTIRE** deck! You will degrease the **whole** kitchen! You will wash **ALL** the plates! And you will peel **ALL** those potatoes! **UNDERSTAND?!**"

I nodded. What else could I do?

"And that's not the end of it!" He sneered. "You'll also have to make the beds (ha, ha, ha!) and fold the sails (hee, hee, hee!). But first, it's time to clean the toilets (ho, ho, ho!)."

I sighed. What else could I do?

"Which way to the toilets?" I asked.

"Ha, ha, ha! That's easy!" he cried. "Just **follow** the stench!"

The Ship of Secrets

1. TELESCOPE ROOM
2. CAPTAIN'S CABIN
3. CAPTAIN'S DINING QUARTERS
4. GALLEY
5. KITCHEN
6. ARMORY
7. CREW CAFETERIA
8. CREW DORMITORY
9. PRISON
10. BATHROOM
11. HOLD
12. TREASURE ROOM
13. BRIDGE
14. MAIN MAST

CAPTAIN SHORTTAIL'S CREW

THE COOK'S PARROT
SALTY
No one sleeps as much as he does!

COOK
CHEF GREASYPAW
He specializes in really disgusting recipes.

PETTY OFFICER
COMMANDER BOSSYFUR
His specialty is yelling and giving orders.

HELMSMAN
SQUEAK McCOMPASS
He decides the ship's route each day.

FIRST SAILOR
BRAD BRAWNYWHISKERS
His many muscles make up for his lack of brainpower.

SECOND SAILOR
CHARLIE CHEESEMAN
He'll eat anything, especially cheese!

THIRD SAILOR
WILLIAM WINDYSNOUT
He's very grumpy but an expert at sails.

FOURTH SAILOR
PIERRE PAWMOUTH
He's always saying the wrong thing!

FIFTH SAILOR
NELLY NIMBLEPAWS
He's very small and very agile.

SIXTH SAILOR
LUCAS LAZYBONES
He seems busy but doesn't do anything!

I sighed. Then I grabbed the bucket and the **scrubbing** brush and headed toward the source of the stench. What else could I do?

The closer I got, the more it stank . . .

I had never smelled anything so gross and disgusting in my entire life!

Blech! What a stench!

THE STINKY PIRATE TOILET

Finally, I found myself in front of a wooden door that had been painted black. **CLOTHESPINS** hung nearby, along with a scroll with the following instructions:

Caution! Put a clothespin on your snout before you enter the bathroom, or you'll be sorry!

I quickly put a clothespin on the tip of my snout. But I could still smell the terrible stench!

Oh, how that bathroom reeked! I looked around me and saw that there were clouds of flies, hordes of cockroaches, and **fleas** jumping everywhere! **How awful!**

At the center of the cabin was a toilet with a pirate **SKULL AND CROSSBONES** carved into the lid.

I worked all night long cleaning that **TERRIFYING** bathroom. I don't think anyone had cleaned it in years!

When I finally finished, it was dawn. I sighed with relief and headed to a **CABIN** labeled:

DECKHAND BUNK.

There, I lay down on the cot under a scratchy, flea-infested wool blanket.

I was **worried** about Sweet Melinda. I hoped her sleeping quarters were better than mine! I

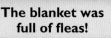

How horrible!

1
The blanket was full of fleas!

Zzzzzzzzz...

2
But I was so tired that I fell fast asleep and began to snore.

knew I had to come up with an **escape** plan, but sleep came first!

Zzzzzz . . . Zzzzzz . . . Zzzzzz . . .

I felt like I had been sleeping for only a few minutes when suddenly . . . **SPLASH!** A bucket of **freezing cold** water hit me in the snout!

It was Chef Greasypaw.

"Wake up, Flycatcher!" he growled. "The sun is already up, and there's a lot of work for you to do today! **UNDERSTAND?!**"

Ahhhh!

3

I was dreaming when a bucket of water hit me in the snout!

He prodded my tail with his enormouse fork, pushing me into the kitchen. A huge **MOUND** of potatoes greeted me.

"Peel! Peel! Peel!" he ordered. *"Got it?!"*

I sighed as he poured himself a glass of mint tea and headed to the deck to **relax**. Meanwhile, I got to work.

I had just started peeling when I heard Captain Shorttail's terrifying shout.

"EVERYONE TO THEIR POSTS! ANCHORS AWEIGH!"

he hollered.

The sailors began to raise the sails while they sang:

"OH, HEAVE-HO AND HOIST! HEAVE-HO AND HOIST! HEAVE-HO AND HOIST!"

A second later, the floor underneath me began to shake.

I looked out the kitchen's PORTHOLE and saw that the sails of the ship were puffed up with air. A second later, the **Ship of Secrets** lifted above the waves and floated into the air.

WHAT A SPECTACULAR SIGHT!

SAILING ON AIR

Captain Shorttail cackled merrily as the ship sailed through the air.

"Squeak McCompass!" he growled. "Route us toward the **LAND OF THE WHOPPING WIZARD!**"

Then he turned to Melinda.

"We're bringing you to the **WHOPPING WIZARD**!" he explained. "He's used up almost all of the VANILLA DUST we gave him. He needs you to make more for him! In exchange, the Whopping Wizard will share his vanilla dust with me so that the *Ship of Secrets* will **fly forever**!

Poor Melinda!

"Don't worry!" I told her. "We'll think of a way out of this SCARY situation. RODENT'S HONOR!"

"Captain Shorttail, you are the *meanest*, most *evil*, most **ferocious** pirate in the Kingdom of Fantasy!" Chef Greasypaw said admiringly.

"Do you think so?" Captain Shorttail replied proudly.

"Yes, you're the best — we mean, the **worst**!" the pirates all cried together.

Ha, ha, ha!

Yo, ho, ho!

You're the worst!

"Well, some say the Whopping Wizard is even **SCARIER** and more **evil** than you, Captain," Pierre Pawmouth squeaked. As soon as he had said it, he clapped his paw over his mouth.

"What did you say?" Captain Shorttail thundered. His fur turned **PURPLE** with rage.

"Blimey!" Nelly Nimblepaws said. "He didn't **mean it**, Captain!"

"Yeah, don't get **ANGRY**, boss," William Windysnout added.

I was watching the pirates argue from the kitchen window. **Rancid ricotta!** I had to think of a plan to **save myself** — and Princess Melinda!

For days and days, we sailed through the sky. I tried to speak with Melinda every day, but Captain Shorttail had ordered Brad Brawnywhiskers to act as her **bodyguard** at all times. I couldn't get in one **squeak!**

One afternoon, we docked the ship in a hidden

bay so the crew could take a rest. Just before sunset, Brad Brawnywhiskers **dozed** off while leaning against the main mast.

"Psst, Flycatcher!" Melinda called. "Um, I mean, Sir Geronimo! Do you have a **plan** yet?"

I tried to reassure her. "I'm working on it, PRINCESS!" I squeaked. "I just know I'll come up with something soon. Rodent's honor!"

Zzzz . . . Zzzzz . . .

Psst, Flycatcher!

You're Shark Meat!

Despite my reassurances, Sweet Melinda still looked down in the snout.

"Do you really think you can **SAVE** us, Knight?" she asked. "I've heard the Whopping Wizard is very powerful, and even **SCARIER** than Captain Shorttail! We're running out of time!"

"Of course I can save us!" I squeaked. I didn't know how I would do it, but I had to say **SOMETHING** to make Melinda feel better. She looked so **UNHAPPY**!

"I'm a brave mouse who is friends with *Queen Blossom*! I'm not afraid of the **WHOPPING WIZARD**!" I continued boastfully. "And I'm not afraid of a **SILLY** little pirate like Captain Shorttail, either!"

Suddenly, I heard a sound behind me. Of course it was CAPTAIN SHORRTAIL!

I spun around. He snarled at me ferociously.

"Well, well, well," Captain Shorttail chuckled. "What do we have here? It's Flycatcher the deckhand. Turns out he's friends with Queen Blossom, an enemy of the Whopping Wizard! Oh, and he's not afraid of anything or anyone, not even a ferocious pirate like me!"

"Flycatcher, you're shark meat!" the pirate crew cried. Then they began to sing:

"FLYCATCHER, YOU LITTLE SCALLYWAG,
YOU SURE PICKED THE WRONG TIME TO BRAG!
MICE LIKE YOU MUST WALK THE PLANK,
AND DIVE RIGHT IN TO THE GREAT SHARK TANK!
HEAVE-HO, LOOK OUT BELOW,
THOSE TEETH ARE SHARP—YO, HO, HO!"

Island of a Thousand Anchors

1. BAY OF SHARP TEETH
2. SLIMY ALGAE STRAIGHTS
3. LURKING PIRATE COVE
4. SEA OF SHARKS
5. WAVING FLAG BAY
6. ABYSS OF SUNKEN
   TREASURE

I looked out at the sea and went pale. The waves roiled with **huge sharks** with open mouths full of *RAZOR-SHARP* teeth!

Moldy mozzarella, that's why it's called the **BAY OF SHARP TEETH**!

I turned to face Captain Shorttail.

"D-dear C-captain," I stuttered. "Yes, of course I know Blossom, but regarding the Whopping Wizard, well, I haven't yet had the **pleasure** of meeting him! Maybe he and I will become **BEST FRIENDS**! And as for being a courageous mouse, well, I'm actually not very **BRAVE**. Come to think of it, I'm **REALLY** not much of a swimmer, either . . ."

The pirates **ignored** me. Brad Brawnywhiskers tied me up and blindfolded me with a stinky bandanna. Then Chef Greasypaw prodded me onto the plank with his sharp, pointy **FORK**!

"Hurry up, Flycatcher!" he snarled. "The sharks

don't like to wait for their **dinner**!"

"Caw!" Salty squawked in agreement.

I trembled in fear as I walked out to the tip of the plank.

"HEEEEEEEEEELP!
I DON'T WANT TO BE SHARK FOOD!"

I cried.

"Too late, rodent!" Captain Shorttail replied. "In a little bit, they will **chew up** your fur and bones. Tee, hee, hee! These sharks just adore mouse meat!"

"*NOOOOOOOO!*" I cried as I fell off the plank. **What a way to go!**

THE BRIGADE OF CURIOUS SEAGULLS

Just as I was about to land in the icy water, I heard a strange sound.

"Squawk! Quick, catch that mouse by the tail. Squawk!"

A second later, a pointy beak grabbed me by the tail and

LIFTED ME INTO THE AIR.

I was still blindfolded,
so I couldn't see a thing.
"*Heeeeeeelp!*"
I squeaked.

What was happening? Was I
being rescued? Or was I being
mousenapped?

A webbed foot pushed the blindfold
off my eyes. I saw that I was
dangling in midair
thanks to a group of **seagulls**!
They flew around me in a giant flock.

The birds squawked in a chorus:
"Don't be afraid, Knight!
You're under the protection of
the BRIGADE OF CURIOUS
SEAGULLS! Squawk! Squawk!
Squawk!"

The seagulls carried me through the sky for

Squawk!

Squawk!

Squawk!

Squawk!

Squawk!

Squawk!

GAME
How many
seagulls can
you count?

Solution: There are thirty-six seagulls.

the entire night. The next morning, we finally **LANDED** on a beach.

"Thank you!" I said gratefully. "You saved me!"

A seagull wearing a GOLD CROWN on his head replied for everyone.

"My name is *Seafeathers the Eighth*," he said. "I am the king of the Curious Seagulls. It was our pleasure to **SAVE YOU**, Knight!"

Thank you!

It was our pleasure!

Seafeathers XIII,
King of the Curious Seagulls

JOKER GULL

STRONG GULL

FUNNY GULL

SINGING GULL

ELEGANT GULL

EXPLORER GULL

CHEF GULL

FANCY GULL

SWIMMING GULL

The Tale of the Curious Seagulls

The Curious Seagulls are some of Blossom's best friends. Many years ago, Queen Blossom saved their ancestor, King Seafeathers the First. One day, while she was out walking along the beach, Blossom found a seagull's nest that had been badly battered in a storm. There were two eggs inside. Blossom brought them to Crystal Castle, where she lovingly cared for them. When the eggs hatched, two seagulls were born. They became the next king and queen of the Curious Seagulls! Today there are thousands of birds in the Brigade of Curious Seagulls.

SEAGULL ATTACK!

"King Seafeathers, how did you know I was in DANGER?" I asked curiously.

"Squawk! You're famouse in the *Kingdom of Fantasy*, Knight!" King Seafeathers explained. "You've already saved our beloved Queen Blossom time and time again. The Curious Seagulls are the sentinels of the sea. Nothing that happens among the waves gets past us — we know all about it! So when we saw that the pirates were about to turn you into shark food, we dove down to save you."

"Yes, it was the perfect **rescue mission,**" the king's wife added. "And thank goodness, because in another second, the sharks would have **devoured** your tail!"

I shivered at that thought. What a close call!

I immediately thought of Sweet Melinda. The pirates were still holding her *captive*!

"Friends, there's another life in danger on that boat — **Sweet Melinda, Princess of the Vanilla Fairies**!" I told the seagulls. "Please help me save her. Together, I know we can do it!"

"But of course!" King Seafeathers cawed solemnly. "I should have figured that out myself when I smelled **vanilla** mixed in with the stench of the **Ship of Secrets**! Seagulls, prepare for another *RESCUE*!"

The seagulls began to run **HERE** and *there*, giving orders right and left.

The princess is in danger!

"PATROL FORMATION!" one squawked.

"No, everyone in line first!" another argued.

"Prepare for the **OPEN-CLAW MANEUVER**," a third cawed.

"It's time for the triple-corkscrew plunge and the pluck-a-feather pirouette!" a fourth seagull shouted gleefully.

Then they all cawed together:

"SEAGULL ATTAAAAAAAAACK!"

The birds launched into flight and headed back toward the Ship of Secrets. They flew in the shape of a **COLOSSAL SEAGULL** with an open beak. As soon as they saw the ship, they dove down at top speed, crying:

"SQUAAAAAAAAKKWK!"

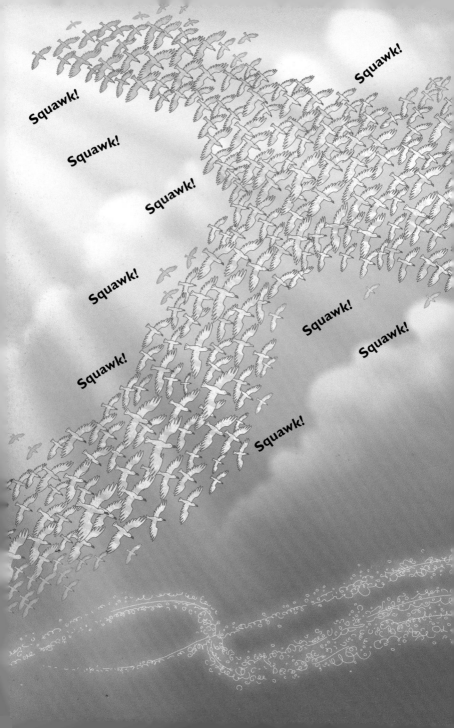

FRIENDS FOREVER!

"**SWASHBUCKLING SWORDS!**" the pirates on the deck shrieked.

"Saaaave yourselves! Retreeeeat!"

A second later, the seagulls swept Princess Melinda into the air and flew her away from the *Ship of Secrets* to safety. The great flock of **SEAGULLS** descended onto the beach and placed Melinda down gently on the sand.

Squawk!

Squawk!

Squawk!

The fairy looked stunned by what had happened.

"Don't worry, Princess!" I reassured her. "These are the Curious Seagulls, and they are our friends!"

"Yes, we're your friends forever!" the seagulls squawked in reply. "And you're our f-r-i-e-n-d, friend!"

Then they began to dance and sing, waving their wings and SQUAWKING cheerfully.

Melinda smiled and clapped her paws with delight at the seagull's FUNNY song.

Squawk!

Squawk!

"**F** means together **f**orever,
R as in **r**eady for whatever,
I like **I**'ll be here always,
E means **e**ven on your worse days,
N like you **n**ever have to be alone
D as in just **d**ial me on the phone!
SQUAAAAWKK!"

"How can I ever thank you, Knight?" she asked, her blue eyes brimming with tears. "When I called on you to come to the *Kingdom of Fantasy*, I knew you would try to help me, but I didn't think your life would be in **DANGER**! When I saw those pirates push you out to the **edge** of that plank, I was afraid all was lost!"

"Don't thank me, thank the seagulls!" I said. "I, too, thought all was LOST, but the seagulls really saved our tails! Now that we've escaped from the pirates, I would love to visit your friend *Blossom* so I can say hello. Maybe she can also help me get back to Mouse Island. My friend Creepella is probably wondering where I disappeared to! She's a little high-strung, and I'm afraid she has a TERRIBLE habit of trying to bonk me in the snout with her purse when she's upset . . ."

"Oh no!" Sweet Melinda replied. "I think Blossom can HELP. And I would love to see her myself. I can't wait to hug my dear friend!"

"It would be our PLEASURE to accompany you both to the Kingdom of the Fairies," King Seafeathers told us. "Blossom is our friend, too, and we haven't seen her in AGES! But first let's have a seafood feast to celebrate our new friendship!"

The seagulls pulled out a **red-and-white-checkered** tablecloth and spread it across the sand. Then the seagull chef fluttered toward us, holding a large tureen in his beak. It was full of steamy, hot, delicious FISH SOUP.

The seagulls gave us CUPS made of shells and carved mother-of-pearl **spoons**. Then they sprinkled sea salt on the soup and squawked a happy little song:

"Now it's time to eat!
Our fish soup can't be beat!
So go ahead and slurp it up,
There's plenty more to fill your cup!"

Once we were finished eating, we prepared for our journey to Queen Blossom's CRYSTAL CASTLE.

Squawk!

There's Crystal Castle!

King Seafeathers and the other curious seagulls constructed an **ENORMOUSE** woven nest to hold Princess Melinda and me. Then they braided **SUPERSTRONG** ropes out of algae and tied those to the nest! They lifted the nest by the ropes and carried us through the **sky** toward CRYSTAL CASTLE. We traveled all day and all night in this **UNIQUE** contraption!

We **flew** very high, but I wasn't scared because I knew that all of our seagull *friends* were watching over us!

A Special Reunion

The seagulls placed the nest **GENTLY** on the roof of Crystal Castle, and Melinda and I hopped out. As we thanked the seagulls for their help, someone I knew very well scampered up to us. It was my friend Scribblehopper the frog! He was accompanied by two other friends — Boils the chameleon and Chatterclaws the crab.

"Knight!" Scribblehopper croaked breathlessly. "Listen up! We have a really, really big problem —"

"Yeah, it's really **BIG**!" Boils interjected. "Let me tell him about it. I'll explain it **BETTER**! Knight, it's a problem only you can —"

"Wait a second!" Chatterclaws shouted, interrupting both of them. "I'll tell him about the thingamabob. I mean, the whatchamacallit. You know, the really gigantic **problem**!"

At that moment, a fourth voice joined the chorus. This voice was soft and sweet.

"Friends, let's give the knight a chance to **rest** for a minute. He must be tired from his trip. There's still time to explain the **TERRIBLE** problems facing the citizens of the Kingdom of Fantasy and ask for his help."

Scribblehopper

Boils

Chatterclaws

I turned to face the most beautiful fairy in the world: Queen Blossom!

The Queen of the Fairies had **LONG** hair that was as **BLUE** as the summer sky and eyes the color of bluebells. Her wings fluttered delicately behind her, and she was wearing a long, rustling silk dress. She wore a crown of roses on her head, and CRYSTAL SLIPPERS on her feet.

Queen Blossom
Queen of the
Kingdom of Fantasy

The Kingdom of Fantasy

1. LAND OF INVISIBLE SPIDERS
2. EMPIRE OF THE RUBY DRAGONS
3. KINGDOM OF THE HISSING SERPENTS
4. LAND OF A THOUSAND SHADOWS
5. LAND OF NIGHTMARES
6. KINGDOM OF THE FIRE DRAGONS
7. KINGDOM OF THE PIXIES
8. KINGDOM OF THE GNOMES
9. KINGDOM OF THE FAIRIES
10. KINGDOM OF THE SEA
11. RAINBOW VALLEY
12. THE TALKING FOREST
13. KINGDOM OF THE NORTHERN GIANTS
14. KINGDOM OF THE ELVES
15. KINGDOM OF THE DIGGERTS
16. LAND OF THE TROLLS
17. KINGDOM OF THE WITCHES
18. LAND OF SWEETS
19. LAND OF THE OGRES
20. KINGDOM OF THE SOUTHERN GIANTS
21. LAND OF TIME
22. KINGDOM OF THE SILVER DRAGONS
23. REALM OF THE TOWERING PEAKS
24. LAND OF TOYS
25. GREEN COUNTY
26. BRIGHT EMPIRE
27. ISLAND OF A THOUSAND BEGINNINGS
28. KINGDOM OF THE GOLDEN GNOMES
29. LAND OF THE FLAMES
30. COUNTY OF THE BLUE WEASELS
31. LAND OF THE WHOPPING WIZARD
32. THE VANILLA ISLANDS

1. ROSE OF A THOUSAND PETALS
2. GLITTERING LAKE
3. WOODS OF GOODNESS
4. PRETTY-SHADE PLAIN
5. PINK FOREST
6. TURQUOISE HOUSE
7. FLOWERY MOUNTAIN
8. TOOTH FAIRY'S MANOR
9. FOUNTAIN OF YOUTH
10. SILVER ABYSS
11. FAIRY GODMOTHER'S TOWER
12. MOUNTAIN OF SWEET DREAMS
13. MOUNTAIN OF SECRETS
14. CRYSTAL CASTLE
15. SWEETWATER LAKE
16. BRIGHT HOPES WAY
17. GREEN GATE
18. FAIRY QUARTER
19. HAPPY TRAILS STATION
20. GAZEBO OF LOVE
21. PETAL WAY
22. FOREST OF THE NYMPHS

The Kingdom of the Fairies

A Fairy's Tears

I knelt down before Queen Blossom and kissed her hand, which smelled like roses.

"My queen, it's so wonderful to see you again," I greeted her. "I'm so glad I'm able to see you before I RETURN HOME!"

She smiled, but her eyes were very worried.

"Knight, I wish I didn't have to do this, but I'm afraid I have to ask for your HELP again!" she said sadly.

"What is it, Queen Blossom?" I asked, concerned.

"I'm in trouble, Knight," she admitted. "I need to ask you to stay here in the Kingdom of Fantasy a little longer."

I hesitated. On the one PAW, of course I wanted to help. But on the other PAW, I knew that **CREEPELLA** was waiting for me back in New Mouse City. Plus, I missed my other friends and family. I was looking forward to seeing them **again**. And I had to get back to work at *The Rodent's Gazette*!

I was **deep** in thought when Princess Melinda **TUGGED** on my shirt impatiently.

"Please say you'll **stay**, Knight!" she implored me.

"Well, of course I'd like to," I mumbled. "But **CREEPELLA** is waiting at the ball . . . and then

Well, there's Creepella . . . and my family . . .

and I have so much work!

there's my family . . . and I have so much work to do at the newspaper . . ."

"Oh, Creepella is such a **nice** name!" Melinda squeaked. "She must be lovely. Is she your girlfriend?"

"No!" I replied, a bit too *QUICKLY*. "I mean, she's just a friend. And, uh, yes, **LOVELY** is one way to, er, describe her. She does have a **STRONG PERSONALITY**!"

Blossom sighed.

"It's not important then, Knight," she said. "Of course you should go home to your *friends* and family! You've already done so much for me and for the Kingdom of Fantasy. It isn't **fair** for me to ask you to do any more!"

"Please, Knight," Melinda whispered. "I beg you to **stay**! If Queen Blossom is asking, it must be **IMPORTANT**!"

Blossom smiled, though her eyes were still sad.

"I won't keep you any longer, Knight," she said. "In fact, if you'd like, I can send you **home** right now."

She raised her ***magic wand***. I knew if she waved it and said the right **spell**, I would return to New Mouse City in the **BLiNK** of an eye.

But then I saw it: A tiny **TEAR** slipped down the queen's cheek.

"Wait!" I cried. "I want to **STAY**! I'll do whatever it takes to help you and the *Kingdom of Fantasy*, Queen Blossom!"

Wait!

"Oh, thank goodmouse," Melinda squeaked happily. "I'm so glad you'll stay!"

Blossom looked directly into my eyes.

"I don't know how to thank you, Sir Geronimo!" she said.

Then she placed her hand on her **heart** and smiled.

"Our **HEARTS** are united," she continued. "They beat together as one, like the hearts of all **friends** who care for each other!"

Our hearts beat together as one . . .

Friendship Friendship

. . . like the hearts of all friends
who care for each other!

THE WIZARD'S
EVIL PLAN

Now that I had decided to stay, I was anxious to find out what the queen needed.

"What can I do for you, Queen Blossom?" I asked.

She showed me a **small black coffer**.

"The Whopping Wizard sent me a letter in this coffer," she explained gravely. "He wants to steal many of the most **precious treasures** in the Kingdom of Fantasy. Then he intends to take over my throne!"

Holey cheese! This wizard sounded scarier than a thousand **HUNGRY** cats!

"Can you tell me more about him?" I asked.

She shook her head.

"I know almost **nothing** about the mysterious

THE WHOPPING WIZARD'S DARK COFFER

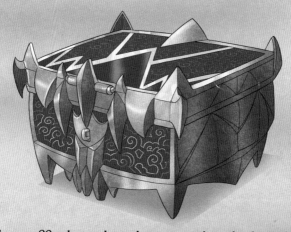

This coffer has a long history: The Black Goblins made it for the witch Scorcher years and years ago. At first, Scorcher kept it at Terror Castle, in the Rotten Valley. Then she gave it to her powerful friend and advisor, the Whopping Wizard. Scorcher had the coffer engraved with the wizard's initials as a sign of her friendship. The wizard used this dark object to send Queen Blossom a terrible letter threatening her and the entire Kingdom of Fantasy!

Whopping Wizard," she explained. "All I know is that he lives in a town near the KINGDOM OF THE SOUTHERN GIANTS and that he's absolutely massive!"

"Not even the largest of the Southern Giants is as tall or as **STRONG** as the Whopping Wizard!" Queen Blossom continued. "And now he has sent me a direct challenge: He intends to **conquer** my kingdom so he can name himself King of the Kingdom of Fantasy! Here, look for yourself . . ."

She opened the coffer and showed me a gray, burned scroll that smelled like smoke. I read it and turned as pale as a slice of mozzarella.

Then I turned to Blossom.

"Tell me, what can I do for you, my queen?" I asked. "Do you want me to travel to all the towns in the Kingdom of Fantasy and let them know that the **WHOPPING WIZARD** has plans to *take over* the kingdom?"

I, the Whopping Wizard, will defeat you!

FIRST: I will steal all of the VANILLA DUST from the Vanilla Islands so I can fly everywhere! Then I will kidnap the PRINCESS OF THE VANILLA FAIRIES and keep her locked in my castle so she can make vanilla dust for me forever and ever!

SECOND: I will steal the TREASURE OF THE GOLDEN GNOMES. Then I'll use the gnomes' gold to build a really tall gold throne. Everyone will know I'm the most POWERFUL wizard in the Kingdom of Fantasy!

THIRD: I will steal the EGG OF FIRE, and I will use it to decorate my crown. Everyone in the Kingdom of Fantasy will be dazzled, and they will honor me as their King!

FOURTH: I will make a gigantic cloak out of precious BLUE WEASEL fur!

THIS IS THE WHOPPING WIZARD'S PROMISE!

THE WHOPPING WIZARD

THE MOST TERRIFYING WIZARD IN THE KINGDOM OF FANTASY

THE SEVEN DRAGONFLY PRINCESSES

Blossom looked me directly in the **EYE**.

"Yes, Knight," she said seriously. "I need you to travel around the kingdom, alerting everyone that the Whopping Wizard could **strike** at any moment. First you must go warn the Golden Gnomes that their precious **gold treasure** is in danger!"

The knight saved me!

He saved me many times, too!

"Of course, my queen!" I replied. "I'll leave as soon as possible."

"WONDERFUL!" Blossom said. "I don't know how to *thank you* for all you've done already."

"But I haven't done anything yet," I said, confused.

"Of **course** you have!" Sweet Melinda replied. "I'm the princess the Whopping Wizard planned to **LOCK** in his castle!"

Queen Blossom hugged Melinda.

"Yes, thank you for saving my **DEAR** friend!" Blossom told me. "You've already partly **foiled** the Whopping Wizard and his **EVIL** plan! But you must leave right away if you want to stop him **AGAIN**. Here is your armor."

She handed it to me, and I put it on.

"I'll call the seven **Dragonfly Princesses**," she continued. "They will drive you around the Kingdom of Fantasy in their **Golden Dragonfly Chariot**."

Then she clapped her hands and the dragonfly princesses **fluttered** into the room.

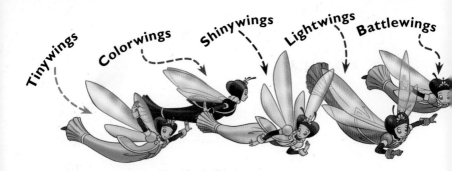

Tinywings Colorwings Shinywings Lightwings Battlewings

"Here we are, quick and lively,
Fluttering through the sky.
We are one; we are many.
We're the seven dragonflies!"

They circled around me, their wings fluttering **cheerfully**.

Just then, I heard Scribblehopper.

"Make way, make way!" the frog cried. "Here comes the **Golden Dragonfly Chariot**!"

A moment later, Scribblehopper pulled an **extraordinary** carriage into the room!

He was accompanied by **Prism** the chameleon, who was serving as flight attendant, and the

Let's go!

Windywings

Violetwings

always-entertaining **Batty Matty**!

Scribblehopper hooked the dragonflies to the carriage and then pushed me aboard.

"Come on, let's go, Knight!" Scribblehopper croaked. "Prepare yourself: This trip is going to have a few **UPS** and a few **DOWNS**, with a **lot** of turbulence in between!"

The Seven Dragonfly Princesses

They reign over the giant dragonflies who live on Sweetwater Lake, next to Crystal Castle. They pull the Golden Dragonfly Chariot, and they will escort Queen Blossom anywhere in the Kingdom.

THE GOLDEN DRAGONFLY CHARIOT

This special chariot was constructed by the most famous jeweler in the Kingdom of Fantasy, Gem Moonstone. It looks like a huge, finely etched dragonfly.

Before the Golden Dragonfly Chariot pulled away, Blossom gave me a precious **RING** decorated with a **magnificent** rose. It was ENGRAVED with Blossom's name in the Fantasian Alphabet.*

"Take this ring, Knight," she told me. "Everyone in the kingdom will recognize my official crest. If anyone doubts you, this ring will help you PROVE that you're traveling in my name!"

I thanked the queen and tucked the ring SAFELY under my armor. A second later, the chariot took off! We were heading straight for the Kingdom of the Golden Gnomes to warn them about the Whopping Wizard!

*You can find the Fantasian Alphabet on page 311.

The Treasure of the Golden Gnomes

For *seven* days and *seven* *nights*, we traveled across that mythical, magical, wonderful golden carriage pulled by the seven **Dragonfly Princesses** . . . As they pulled the Golden Dragonfly Chariot, the princesses sang:

"Here we are, quick and lively,
Fluttering through the sky.
We are one; we are many.
We're the seven dragonflies!
Seven sisters, all princesses,
United by pure hearts.
In harmony we fly together;
We'll never be apart!"

I Don't Want to Be a Mouse Omelet!

It was an extraordinary trip, but it was also very long. I had a **headache** from Prism's chatter and from **Batty Matty's** strange tunes! Plus I was feeling chariotsick from all the **TURBULENCE**.

Prism offered me a **smoothie**.

"No, thanks," I said politely.

"But you'll **love** it, Knight!" Prism insisted. "I added some **red ants** for extra flavor, and some **scorpion saliva** to help with digestion!"

I was already as **GREEN** as a lizard, but just thinking about that smoothie made me turn three shades **DARKER**! Now I really looked like the **FROG PRINCE**!

As the chariot continued to hurtle along at supersonic speeds, Batty Matty started singing about **graves**.

"Oh, oh, toward the cemetery we go,

We're moving so fast — not at all slow!

If we should crash,

It'll happen in a flash,

And we'll share a nice grave down below!"

At dawn on the eighth day, we flew over a wonderful landscape. There were enormouse, wide-open green fields as far as the eye could see. The dragonflies slowed their flight, aiming toward a round hill in the middle of the fields.

"There's our first stop, GOLDEN GRAIN HILL," Scribblehopper cried. "It's the secret entrance to the gnomes' gold mines!

"But if the entrance is a secret, how will we find it?" I asked.

Scribblehopper looked OFFENDED.

"I, Scribblehopper, know EVERYTHING about the Kingdom of Fantasy!" he crowed confidently. "Why else do you think Queen Blossom sent me with you?"

Then he began to *rummage* in his jacket pockets. Finally, he produced a large map that marked the itinerary of our trip.

"Look carefully at this map," he said. "All the **DANGERS** we will confront are marked: ugly ogres, **WITCHES** hungry for fresh mouse meat, castles full of howling ghosts, headless knights, and **TROLLS** with breath so bad it will make you faint.

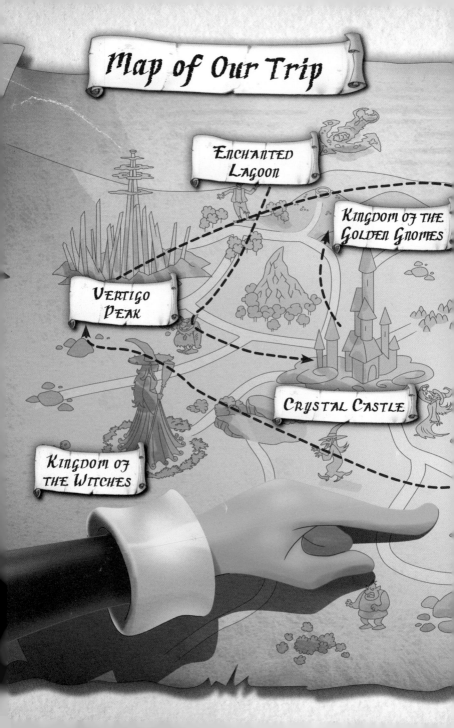

THE VANILLA
ISLANDS

COUNTY OF THE
BLUE WEASELS

LAND OF THE
WHOPPING WIZARD

The dragonflies headed for a **well** at the top of Golden Grain Hill.

"This well is the secret entrance that will take us straight to the gnomes," Scribblehopper revealed. "But we have to hit the exact center of the well, or . . . trust me, you **don't want to know!**"

OH, great Gouda! What if we weren't able to do it? Would we **crash** into the ground?

"T-tell the dragonflies to slow down," I ordered Scribblehopper, my teeth chattering with fear. "I don't want to be a *mouse omelet!*"

"Dear Knight, aren't you supposed to be fearless?" Scribblehopper asked, **incredulous**.

mouse omelet

Yikes!

"Ahem, yes, I guess, well, I suppose I do have a **REPUTATION** for being brave, but . . ."

Scribblehopper **COVERED** his ears.

"Well, then, I'll pretend I didn't hear you begging for your life, as scared as a **rat** caught in a **TRAP**!" Scribblehopper winked at me. "I know you have a reputation to uphold. Your **SECRET** is safe with me!"

I tried to pry his fingers from his ears. When that didn't **work**, I jumped up and down, waving at him *desperately*.

"No, no, no, no, Scribblehopper," I squeaked. "**DON'T WORRY** about my reputation! Worry about what's going to happen to us if this chariot goes **splat**!"

But Scribblehopper was a true **friend**. He thought he was doing me a favor by **NOT LISTENING**! Instead, he began to sing a ridiculous song:

"La, la, I don't hear you.
Oh, Knight, you're so brave!
I really can't hear you,
There's no need to wave!
I'm plugging my ears now,
That's what I must do!
Your secret is safe —
I'm a friend, through and through!"

I can't hear you!

Nooooo!

A second later, the chariot zoomed straight into the black center of the secret entrance.

The Dragonfly Princesses had done it!

At the secret entrance, a large brass eye allows the **GUARDIAN GNOME** to see all visitors wishing to gain access to the gnomes' mine.

FUNNELPHONE ROOM

This room is found at the entrance of the gnomes' mine. The funnelphone is a speaker that is used to communicate with the Guardian Gnome. If he doesn't respond, he's either taking a nap, having a snack, or using the bathroom!

HEY, INTRODUCE YOURSELVES!

Instead of crashing into the ground, the chariot bounced to a gentle stop atop an enormous mountain of very **soft** pillows!

I looked around me, bewildered. The room was perfectly **round**, the floor was covered in **colorful** pillows, and the walls were lined with a **soft** red quilt.

"Hey, you!" a voice cried. "**Introduce yourselves!** I am the Guardian Gnome, and I must know your **names** and where you **come from**. Come on, hurry up! I'm very busy. I don't have *all day*!"

The voice came from the **funnelphone**. This brass funnel was connected to a lens in the shape of an eye. It enabled the Guardian Gnome to see and hear us.

"Are you talking to **us**?" I asked, unsure of myself.

"Of course I am!" the voice **BELLOWED**. "I'm talking to you, the **mouse** and the **FROG**. I can see you very well from here, but I need to know your names and where you're from. **SPEAK UP!** I also need to know who those **dragonflies** are, and who the bat and the chameleon are. I must file an official report on all visitors. *Come on, squeak up, Mouse!*"

Squeak up, Mouse!

Ahhh!

"Yes, of course," I said quickly. "I am Geronimo Stilton,

uh, I mean, *Sir Geronimo of Stilton*. I hail from New Mouse City, and I am on a secret mission on behalf of *Queen Blossom*. My companions are Scribblehopper, a literary frog; **Batty Matty**, a singing bat; Prism, a flight attendant; and the seven Dragonfly Princesses from Sweetwater Lake."

"Yippee!" the Guardian Gnome shouted suddenly. "Are you really the fearless knight who has been sent by Queen Blossom? We've been waiting for you! I'll be right there to let you in!"

A second later, a door in the padded wall opened and we saw the smiling face of a **golden** gnome. He had ROUND cheeks, bushy eyebrows, and a very **long** beard . . . and he was completely gold! He wore a **RED** tunic, a matching **RED** hat with a rolled tip, and BLUE tights with white stripes.

He bowed when he saw me.

"Knight, please forgive me," he said. "I didn't recognize you. I imagined someone taller, stronger, and, well, more FEARLESS-LOOKING than a mouse in glasses! But that doesn't matter — the **important** thing is that you're here. Come in, come in!"

Scribblehopper giggled.

"Ha, ha, ha, Knight," he said. "You see? I'm not the only one who thinks you look a little too scared for a knight!"

THE GOLDEN GNOMES

SANCHO, KING OF THE GOLDEN GNOMES

He was elected because his citizens have great faith in him.

ROSA, QUEEN OF THE GOLDEN GNOMES

Everyone comes to her when they need advice.

FERDINAND, HERBALIST GNOME

He knows all the secret medicinal uses of the plants in the Kingdom of Fantasy.

PABLO, MUSICAL GNOME

He loves to cheer his friends by playing the violin.

ALEX AND YVETTE, CHEF GNOMES

They grow fruits and vegetables in their garden and turn them into delicious dishes.

AURORO, GOLDSMITH GNOME

He creates beautiful gold jewelry.

ARBORIA, GARDENER GNOME

She has an incredible green thumb and can make any plant grow!

CARL, CARPENTER GNOME

He can build almost anything out of wood.

WILLIAM, LITERARY GNOME

He composes poetry about nature.

PENELOPE, ARTIST GNOME

She paints wonderful watercolor paintings.

EMILIA, SEAMSTRESS GNOME

She weaves and sews elegant clothing.

GUARDIAN GNOME

He might seem surly, but he has a heart of gold.

THE GNOME HOME

Scribblehopper and I left Prism, Batty Matty, and the dragonflies in the **funnelphone** room and followed the gnome through the door.

"**The knight is here!**" he yelled at the top of his lungs.

Many gnomes ran to meet us — there were **young** gnomes and **old** gnomes, **LARGE** gnomes and **small** gnomes.

Yay!

Welcome!

Hooray!

"Welcome!" they all yelled as they lifted me up and carried me on their shoulders **JOYFULLY**.

They led me triumphantly down a dark, **CURVY** corridor until we came out in an **immense** underground cave!

The tall rock walls were full of tiny little doors and **LIT WINDOWS**: This is where all the gnomes lived!

When we reached the Throne Room, two gnomes wearing crowns greeted us. The king held a small **GOLDEN PICKAX** in his hand as a symbol of the gnomes' hard work in mining.

The queen held a **GOLDEN NEEDLE**. She

Yeah!

Long live the knight!

Yippee!

Yahoo!

was embroidering a pair of **newborn shoes** with gold thread for her beautiful baby niece Dorothea! The queen rocked the tiny gnome as she slept in a minuscule cradle, surrounded by her affectionate **brothers** and sisters.

I tried to show them the ring with *Blossom's crest* on it, but the king shook his head.

"We don't need the crest, Knight!" he explained. "Your fame precedes you, and you are welcome here. We are Sancho and Rosa, the king and queen of the Golden Gnomes. Now tell us, what brings you here?"

"I'm on a **MISSION** for Queen Blossom," I said. "She wanted me to warn you that the gold in your mines is in **grave danger**!"

"What?!" the gnomes gasped.

SANCHO AND ROSA,
KING AND QUEEN OF THE
GOLDEN GNOMES

"Yes, it's true," Scribblehopper croaked. "The Whopping Wizard has vowed to **steal** all your gold!"

The king and the queen smiled.

"Thank you for traveling here to warn us, Knight," the queen said.

"But the *treasure of the Golden Gnomes* is safe," the king continued. "Follow us and we'll show you!"

Scribblehopper and I followed them along the tunnels that went *DOWN*, *DOWN*, *DOWN* into the mines. We finally arrived at the entrance to the legendary gold mine of the Golden Gnomes!

INSIDE THE
GOLD MINE

Once we went through the **entrance**, we meandered down a very **LONG ROCK TUNNEL**. The walls were studded with enormouse nuggets of

GLEAMING
GOLD.

"These are our gold mines," the king said proudly. "As you can see, this place is full of the purest **GOLD** in the Kingdom of Fantasy!"

We followed him down the narrow, dark, and curvy tunnel. As we walked, we saw many gnomes working cheerfully, **excavating** the gold with pickaxes as they sang in unison.

SONG OF THE GOLDEN GNOMES

Working hard is the way to go,
Not too fast and not too slow.
Side by side we toil together,
No matter the season or the weather!

With love in our hearts,
Mining gold is our art.
Every gnome knows what to do,
To learn how, here's a clue:
Being with friends is the key,
To working together happily.
We stay cheerful all day long,
As we sing our mining song!

The king turned down a narrow corridor to the **left**. We followed him and found ourselves in front of a great GOLDEN gate. Behind the gate was a **DEEP** cave piled high with SHINY, gleaming gold nuggets! What an extraordinary sight!

1. FUNNELPHONE ROOM
2. ENTRANCE TO THE MINE
3. MAIN TUNNEL
4. SECONDARY TUNNEL
5. CARTS FOR MOVING GOLD
6. TRACKS FOR THE CARTS
7. GNOMES AT WORK
8. GNOMES HAVING A SNACK
9. GNOMES TAKING A NAP
10. GNOMES WEIGHING GOLD NUGGETS
11. TREASURE CAVE
12. GNOMES BRINGING NUGGETS TO CAVE
13. PICKAX ROOM
14. LIVING QUARTERS

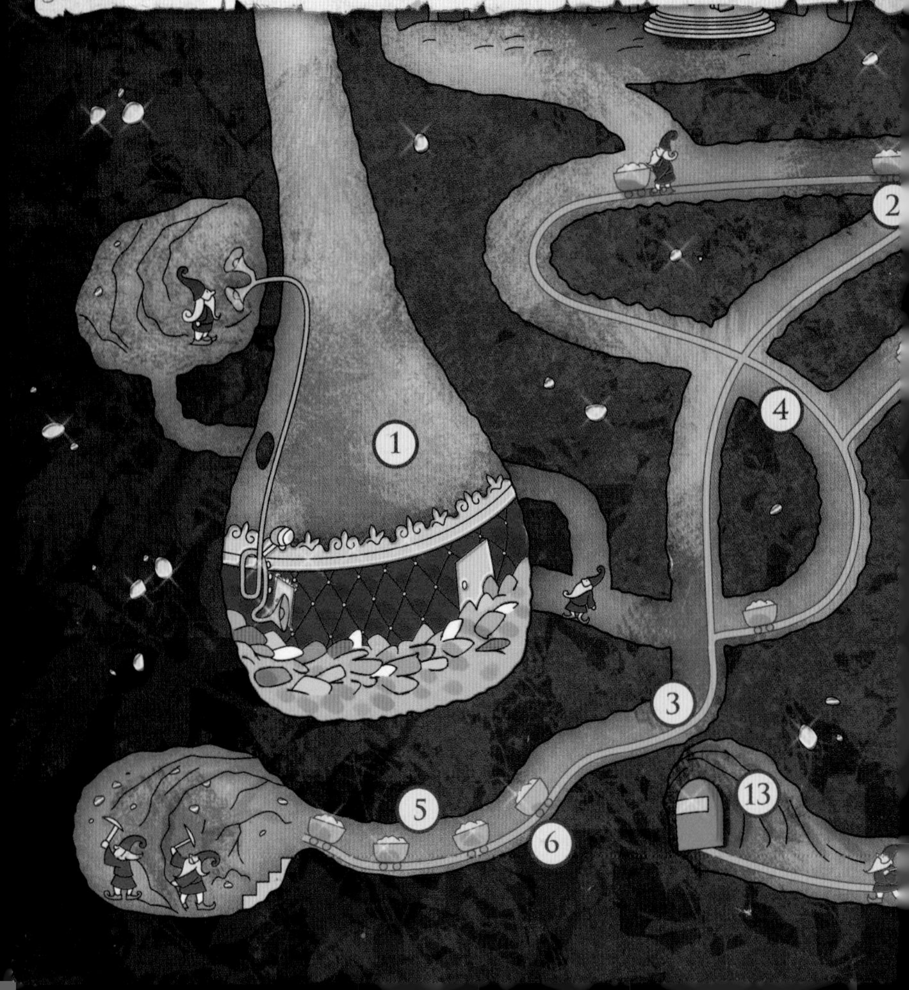

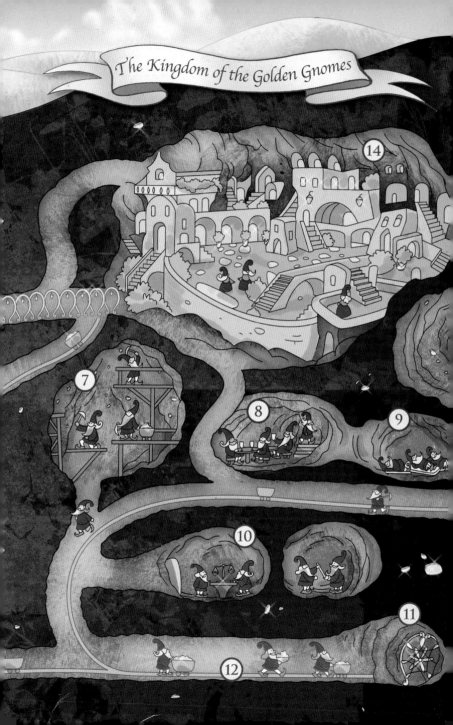

The Kingdom of the Golden Gnomes

WHAT? WHAT? WHAT?

The GOLDEN GATE was as thick as a mouse's fist and fixed securely in the rock. Seven GOLDEN locks held it closed.

The king pointed at the gate.

"See, Knight," he said. "This gate is **STRONG** and impenetrable. See the **SEVEN** locks? Now do you understand why we're not scared of thieves? It's because we're **certain** no one could ever steal the *treasure of the Golden Gnomes*!"

"**Exactly!**" the queen agreed.

"Wow," Scribblehopper croaked, impressed. "Look at all that gold! **It's so shiny!**"

Suddenly, I noticed a strange **stink** in the cave.

"Do you smell algae and **rotten fish**?" I asked the others as I wriggled my nose. "And is that the odor of fresh paint?"

I reached out to touch the golden bars, and I realized it was a canvas that was still wet!

"It's fake!" I shouted. "This is a **PAINTING!**"

What a strange smell!

1 There was a weird odor.

Huh?

2 I touched the bars and realized it was a canvas!

It's fake!

3 There was gold paint on my paw!

189

"What? What? What?" the king shouted in shock. "What do you mean? How could this happen? I don't understand!"

I reached out and **TORE DOWN** the canvas. Everyone gasped. On the other side, the cave was completely EMPTY: The treasure was GONE! Thieves had taken the treasure of the Golden Gnomes!

But how had they done it?

We looked around and soon understood: Someone had **drilled** a hole in the cave ceiling to get into the tunnel undetected. Then the **THIEVES** had broken the gate, entered the mine, and taken the treasure!

The king fainted, dropping to the floor of the cave like a bowling pin.

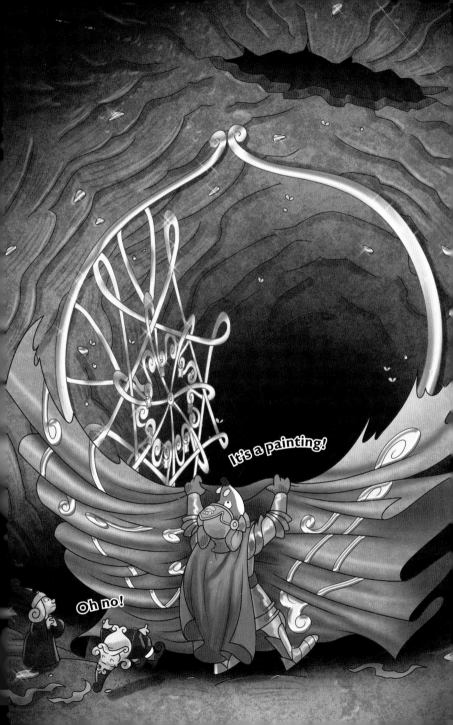

"How will we tell our citizens that the treasure has been stolen?" the queen asked, sobbing. "Oh, woe is me!"

"Don't worry, Queen Rosa!" I said, trying to console her.

"We'll find your gold and return it to you. Rodent's honor!"

Meanwhile, Scribblehopper pulled out a little chalkboard where he had a list of all the TREASURES we were on a mission to protect. Sadly, he made an **X** next to "*treasure of the Golden Gnomes.*"

"**HOW** will we find the gold?" Scribblehopper asked. "We don't even know *who* took it!"

Then I noticed something on the ground in a corner of the cave: There was a heap of **stinky algae** and a FISH BONE. So that's where the

Hmmm . . . stinky algae and a fish bone!

STRANGE smell had come from!

"I know who stole your gold!" I exclaimed. "It was **CAPTAIN SHORTTAIL** and the

PIRATES OF THE SHIP OF SECRETS!"

How terrible! I knew we had to do more to stop the **WHOPPING WIZARD** (and his ally Captain Shorttail) from stealing any more **TREASURES**.

We left the gold mine and returned to the Golden Dragonfly Chariot. It was time to head off for new adventures — and new dangers! With hearts full of **sadness**, we waved good-bye to the king and queen of the Golden Gnomes.

"We'll get your gold back!" I promised.

The Dragonfly Princesses explained that Queen Blossom had called **Prism** and **Batty Matty** back to the Crystal Castle. We would be continuing on our journey without them. I breathed

Sniff! Sniff!

We have to go!

Good-bye!

a *SIGH* of relief. At last I would have some *peace* and QUIET!

Scribblehopper pointed at the horizon.

"Knight, are you ready for the next leg of our journey?" he asked. "We're heading toward

FAREWELL! FAREWELL!

FAREWELL! FAREWELL! FAREWELL!

FAREWELL! FAREWELL!

FAREWELL! FAREWELL!

Vertigo Peak, where a frightening dragon with seven heads watches over the Egg of Fire in a copper-wire nest. Captain Shorttail and his pirates have already stolen the vanilla dust and the *treasure of the Golden Gnomes*, so we have to stop them from getting their paws on the EGG OF FIRE and fur from the Blue Weasels. If Captain Shorttail gives all the stolen treasures to the Whopping Wizard, he will complete his EVIL PLAN to take over the Kingdom of Fantasy!"

I gulped. This journey was really getting SCARY! I held on tightly as the Dragonfly Princesses pulled the Golden Dragonfly Chariot closer and closer to Vertigo Peak.

The Egg of Fire

A NEST OF
COPPER WIRE

Believe it or not, I was so **STRESSED** and **EXHAUSTED** that I fell asleep during our journey. I even started snoring!

"Wake up, wake up, wake up!" Scribblehopper

suddenly shouted in my ear. "Knight, **LOOK** over there! It's Vertigo Peak!"

"Squeak!" I was **jolted** awake. "What is it? Who is it? Where am I?"

Scribblehopper snapped at me: *Snap, snap, snap!*

"Come on, Knight, get with the program!" he croaked. "Were you REALLY sleeping? The treasure of the Golden Gnomes was already **stolen** on our watch. We have to get ready for the *dangers* that await us!"

"Okay, okay!" I replied as I sat up and looked out the window of the chariot.

It was noon and the SCORCHING SUN was shining down on the craggy peak ahead. I saw a landscape of rocks as red as HOT FLAMES. A strange nest made of COPPER WIRE sat at the tippy-top of the tall, twisty mountain peak.

The GOLDEN DRAGONFLY CHARIOT landed at the foot of Vertigo Peak. Scribblehopper pulled out the *Legendarium,* the enormouse manual he wrote about the mysterious places and creatures of the Kingdom of Fantasy. Then he opened the book and pointed to a page that was all about the frighteningly famous Vertigo Peak!

VERTIGO PEAK

Vertigo Peak is found in the Kingdom of the Fire Dragons, the home of Flamefighter, the dragon with seven heads! A large nest made from copper wire sits on the mountain's summit. There, Flamefighter guards the Egg of Fire.

Only one creature at a time may approach the copper nest!

THE DRAGON WITH SEVEN HEADS

Scribblehopper squeezed my paw solemnly.

"**Good luck**, Knight . . . you'll need it!" he said. "If you don't return, it was a pleasure knowing you — at least most of the time! And if you do become **DRAGON FOOD**, don't worry! I'll make sure to get you a nice tombstone. I'll even arrange a *lovely* funeral in your honor. You have a `last will and testament`, right? I hope you left me something good!"

I turned as **PALE** as mozzarella.

"What?" I squeaked, terrified. "What do you mean, **if** I become dragon food? Of course I won't! Will I?"

"Hey, you never know," Scribblehopper replied with a shrug. "And I figured I'd say good-bye now since you have to go on from here **ALL ALONE**."

He pointed to the sentence in small print in the *Legendarium*: "Only one creature at a time may approach the copper nest!"

Then he pushed me toward the peak.

Good-bye, Knight! Good luck!

There you go!

"Go ahead, Knight!" he said encouragingly. "Be **BRAVE**! I know you can do it!"

The dragonflies said good-bye with tears in their eyes.

"If we could go with you, **WE WOULD**!" they said sweetly. "Best of luck to you, Knight!"

I raised my head and stared up, up, up at the very high peak. My fur **curled** with fear.

SQUEAK! I WAS REALLY IN TROUBLE!

But I had no choice, so I took a deep breath and began to climb. Slowly, I made my way up the **steep** stone staircase that wrapped around Vertigo Peak. At one point I stopped for a second and looked **DOWN**: What a mistake!

My paws were trembling so much I had to flatten myself against the side of the mountain like a slice of Swiss on a sandwich!

Scribblehopper shouted at me from below.

"You aren't thinking of **turning back**, are you, Knight?" he croaked. "Think about Queen Blossom! Don't let her down!"

I finally arrived at the top of Vertigo Peak. I carefully stepped into the copper nest. At its center was a large, sparkling egg: It was the

EGG
OF
FIRE!

Squeak!

Fascinated, I reached out a paw to **touch** it. A moment later, a cloud moved in front of the sun, **BLOCKING** its light.

Cheese niblets! I realized too late that it wasn't a cloud . . . It was a **fire-breathing dragon with seven heads**! When he saw me near the egg, he roared **FEROCIOUSLY** from each head: **"ROAR! ROAR! ROAR! ROAR! ROAR! ROAR! ROAR!"**

Then he dove toward me, shooting **NIGHTMARISH** flames from each of his seven mouths!

IN THE COPPER NEST

When the dragon moved closer, I took a better look: He was a **GIGANTIC** creature with a muscular body covered in **shiny** red scales as bright as rubies. The dragon had wings of fire on his back and very sharp **CLAWS** on his feet. He had seven large heads and seven mouths full of **RAZOR-SHARP** teeth. And he stared at me with fourteen **penetrating** eyes.

Flamefighter landed in the nest and squatted on the egg, clutching it between his claws. He

FLAMEFIGHTER'S STORY

Flamefighter is a Fire Dragon descended from the fearsome Dragons with Seven Heads. He's an unpredictable dragon with a very short temper: He often spits fire for no reason! He was chosen to guard his clan's last Egg of Fire because of his ferocious and terrifying character. Only he knows how to guard and defend the egg. If the egg winds up in the wrong hands or is destroyed, the noble clan of the Dragons with Seven Heads will become extinct.

opened his seven mouths (which were full of **RAZOR-SHARP** teeth!) and began to sing with a deep voice that made me shiver with fright:

"What are you doing in my sacred nest?
Don't you dare try to steal my egg, you pest!"

"Um, excuse me, Sir Flamefighter." I tried **frantically** to explain myself. "I am Sir Geronimo of Stilton, and I'm a knight, not a **THIEF**! In fact, I'm here to tell you that Captain Shorttail and his crew of **evil pirates** are on their way here on their flying **Ship of Secrets**. They're the ones who want to take the Egg of Fire!"

I paused to catch my breath. Flamefighter just **STARED** at me with his fourteen eyes.

"Maybe you don't **believe** me," I continued nervously. "I can see from your expression that, uh, I'll have to convince you! **SQUEAK!**"

Thin lines of **SMOKE** poured out of Firefighter's fourteen nostrils. Then he opened his seven mouths to respond in verse:

"So you are the legendary knight, I see. How can I be sure you are trustworthy?"

My whiskers trembled and my fur curled with fear. Oh, I was so scared!

Then I had an idea.

"Wait a moment, Mr. Flamefighter," I replied. "I can show you the ring with *Blossom's crest* on it . . ."

The dragon snorted:

"Show it to me quickly, before you are toast. If you're lying, beware: I love a good mouse roast!"

I pulled out the ring from under my armor with trembling paws and gave it to him. He examined it for what felt like an ETERNITY! Finally, he sang again:

"Knight, it's a lucky day for you. It seems that what you say is true!"

Here is the ring with Blossom's crest!

I breathed a sigh of **RELIEF**. Then the dragon sang again:

"You say these pirates have a ship that flies? And that they travel through the skies?"

"Yes, it's true," I replied.

Flamefighter looked **worried**.

"I thought this peak was quite secure. But from above, they'll get the egg for sure!"

I tried to think of a way to ⯃⯃⯃𝙴𝙻𝙿.

"Mr. Flamefighter," I said tentatively, "maybe I can take the egg to Queen Blossom for you. She will keep it safe until the **danger** has passed!"

The **DRAGON** stared at the egg with 𝐓𝐄𝐀𝐑𝐒 in his fourteen eyes.

"Alas, I do not want to let it go. But in my heart, I know it must be so!"

Then he gently placed the egg inside a 𝙢𝙖𝙜𝙞𝙘 𝙘𝙝𝙚𝙨𝙩 and gave it to me.

I'll take care of it!

THAT'S NOT
A GOOD IDEA!

I hurried down to the base of Vertigo Peak, the
chest clutched in my paws. Scribblehopper and
the Dragonfly Princesses were waiting for me.

"Good job, **KNIGHT**!" the dragonflies cheered.
Scribblehopper was less generous.

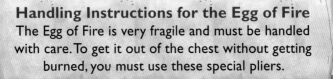

Handling Instructions for the Egg of Fire
The Egg of Fire is very fragile and must be handled
with care. To get it out of the chest without getting
burned, you must use these special pliers.

"It took you long enough, Knight," he grumbled. "Come on, let's go! Our next stop is the County of the Blue Weasels."

We climbed into the Golden Dragonfly Chariot and the dragonflies began to fly northeast. The air became **colder** and **colder**, and the wind grew **STRONGER** and **STRONGER**. My fur began to **freeze** from the tips of my whiskers to the end of my tail!

We traveled for a long time, past sunset.

The full moon sparkled beautifully in the chilly night sky!

Finally, the dragonflies landed the chariot along the banks of a *FAST-MOVING* river.

"We'll sleep here **tonight**!" Scribblehopper announced.

It was really, COLD, and

We'll sleep here!

we wanted to light a fire to warm us. But we didn't have anything to **BURN**!

OH, IT WAS SO COLD!

My fur was frozen, my teeth wouldn't stop **CHATTERING**, and my tail was a giant **icicle**!

Suddenly, I had an idea.

"We can warm ourselves using the **EGG OF FIRE**!" I exclaimed.

"No, Knight!" Scribblehopper said. "Don't take the egg out. It could be very **DANGEROUS**!"

The seven dragonflies nodded in agreement. "That's not a **GOOD IDEA**, Knight!" they said.

"Relax!" I said. "We're all alone here. And it's **freezing**! What's the harm?"

Before they could stop me, I ran to the chariot and opened the **magic chest**. A puff of smoke came out.

I used the special pliers to carefully remove the

scorching-hot egg. Then I placed it gently on the ground in front of us.

Ah! I held my paws over the egg.

"Feel how **toasty warm** it is, friends!" I said.

"I really don't think this is a **good idea**!" Scribblehopper repeated nervously as he hopped from one foot to another.

But it was too late.

Suddenly, I heard a **rustling** sound overhead, and I smelled a strange and terrible **stench**.

I looked up and saw the **Ship of Secrets** soaring through the air above us! The sails of the ship were full of wind, and Captain Shorttail's crew ran here and there across the ship's deck.

"Over here — no over there!" Captain Shorttail yelled.

"GET BUSY, FOOLS, OR I'LL THROW YOU IN THE SEA WITH THE SHARKS!"

My fur bristled when he mentioned the sharks. **Squeak!**

Then I heard a metallic sound:

CLANG, CLANG, CLANG!

Hee, hee, hee!

A **thick metal chain** with a fat anchor on the end descended from the deck of the ship above us. Can you guess who was dangling from the anchor?

It was Captain Sammy Shorttail in the fur and whiskers, of course!

He was holding an enormouse pair of PLIERS, which he used to grab the Egg of Fire!

"Noooooooo!" I cried desperately, trying to stop him.

But he was STRONGER AND FASTER than me. With a triumphant laugh, he snatched the egg away.

"Hee, hee, hee!" he cackled. "The Egg of Fire is mine, ALL MINE!"

As fast as the wind, he zipped back up onto the Ship of Secrets, clinging to the anchor.

The ship FLOATED up high into the sky, its sails straining in the wind. Captain Shorttail steered toward the stars, taking the precious Egg of Fire with him!

I stood there staring at the Ship of Secrets as it flew away, my heart full of SADNESS.

"Leaping lily pads!" Scribblehopper shouted. "I warned you, Knight. But you didn't listen to me!"

I warned you!

I'm so sorry!

Cheer up, Knight!

Then Scribblehopper got out his chalkboard with the list of the treasures we were supposed to be PROTECTING. He added another **X**, this time next to the "EGG OF FIRE."

"Oh, this is going very, very **BADLY**!" Scribblehopper said with a sigh. "I expected **more** from a brave and courageous knight!"

I hung my head, **EMBARRASSED**. I had disappointed Scribblehopper and let down Queen Blossom and the entire Kingdom of Fantasy!

But the dragonflies encouraged me to go on.

"Cheer up, Knight!" they said gently. "You can still make things right. Just keep your snout up and *be brave*. Don't give up now!"

I smiled and thanked them. If the Dragonfly Princesses had faith in me, then I knew I could do it!

We quietly climbed back aboard the Golden Dragonfly Chariot and took off toward the next stop on our adventure, the **County of the Blue Weasels**! Who knew what we would find there? I hoped it wouldn't be too **SCARY**. The less scary it was there, the better chance I had of actually being brave and courageous, like a **REAL** knight!

I really didn't want to **disappoint** Queen Blossom. And the treasure of the Blue Weasels was truly **special** . . . it was the weasels' *beautiful* and **DELICATE** fur. I had to keep the Blue Weasels safe!

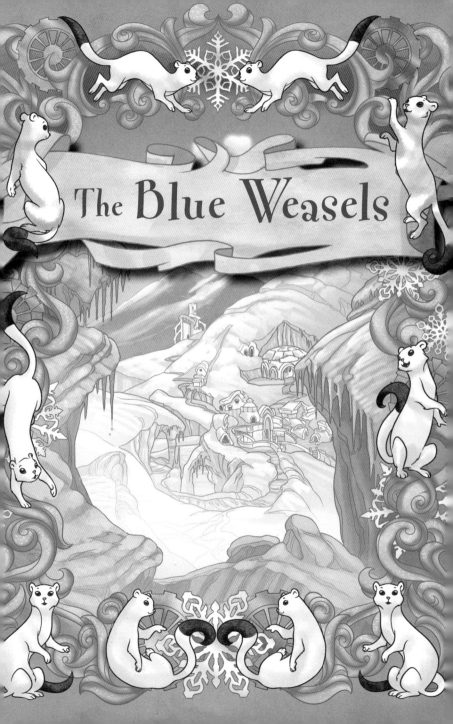

The Blue Weasels

THE DOOR TO ETERNAL WINTER

We flew for miles and miles until we saw an INCREDIBLE sight on the horizon. All around us the landscape was lush, green, and full of flowers. But ahead of us was an ice-covered portal into a frosty world of snow and ice. Although it was spring all around us, the door ahead seemed to lead us straight into winter!

As we approached the portal, the dragonflies slowed down, shocked and amazed by the landscape that lay ahead.

"Leaping lily pads, we did it!" Scribblehopper shouted. "That's the legendary DOOR TO ETERNAL WINTER. Once we fly through it, we will enter the County of the Blue Weasels! I've heard legends about it for years, but I've never seen it before.

Twisting tadpoles, how **incredible**!"

He pulled out the *Legendarium*. Then he turned to page 313.

"Here it is!" he croaked with excitement. "Read all about it, Knight. You should know all about the **County of the Blue Weasels** so you're prepared. You're about to **freeze** your tail off! And based on the way you handled the cold back there with the **EGG OF FIRE**, well, I can tell you're **WEAK** when it comes to **WINTER**!"

He handed me the book, and I read the page aloud so the dragonflies could hear, too. What an **AMAZING** tale!

The dragonflies seemed anxious about flying through the **ICY** portal. They fluttered their wings **nervously** as we hovered just on the other side of the door.

"Don't worry, dragonflies," Scribblehopper

THE DOOR TO ETERNAL WINTER

The Door to Eternal Winter is found in the far eastern part of the Kingdom of Fantasy. Few travelers have gone through it, and even fewer have returned to tell their adventures! The cold there is terrible because the seasons never change — it's always winter! Every day of the year is icy, snowy, and really, really frigid.

Very few plants are able to survive in these difficult conditions: Only mosses, lichens, and small bushes can grow. The only animals that live there are the Blue Weasels. They are famous for their very thick, very soft, and very shiny white fur. Their fur is so white that it almost appears blue in the sunlight, which is how they got their name.

Phew!

The Dragonflies grew more and more tired.

Brrrrr!

I grew colder and colder ...

It's so chilly!

Even Scribblehopper was freezing!

reassured them. "We'll be okay! We're almost there — it's just a little **farther**!"

So the dragonflies beat their wings harder and we sailed through the opening. The temperature dropped immediately, the sky **clouded over**, and snowflakes began to fall. The wind howled and blew ferociously as the landscape became **whiter** and **whiter**.

We continued to fly for hours, and the **dragonflies** grew more and more tired as I grew **colder** and **colder**.

The only good thing was that Scribblehopper was very, very **quiet**: He didn't dare open his mouth because he was AFRAID HIS TONGUE WOULD FREEZE!

We flew **DEEPER** and **DEEPER** into that frigid white land, looking for someone who could tell us **WHERE** we were and how much farther it was to get to the Blue Weasels. But from above, we didn't see **ANYONE**. The only thing keeping us **alive** was the fact that the Golden Dragonfly Chariot was full of **soft**, cozy sweaters and warm, fluffy blankets that kept us as **warm** as possible, like BIRDS IN A NEST! The Dragonfly Princesses wore **thick** wool jackets so they could withstand the COLD, too.

Thank goodmouse for the Dragonfly Princesses and their Golden Dragonfly Chariot! Without them, we would never have made it all the way across that barren, frozen landscape!

That's better!

A VILLAGE OF ICE

We finally spotted a valley below us with a village of tiny ice houses. As we flew closer, we looked for signs of life. But there were NONE!

IT SEEMED LIKE A VILLAGE OF GHOSTS!

"In the name of Queen Blossom, is anyone home?" Scibblehopper shouted as we flew by.

But the only reply was a giant echo:

"HOME? HOME? HOME? HOME?"

Scribblehopper sighed.

"Knight, I officially inform you that this village is unfortunately

ABSOLUTELY . . .

COMPLETELY . . .

TOTALLY . . .

UNINHABITED!"

I shivered. Yes, I was **COLD**. But I was also really, really *SCARED*! What in the name of cheese were we going to do now? We were all alone in a frozen land, with **NO IDEA** where to turn next! Chattering cheddar, how had I gotten myself into this mess?

The County of the Blue Weasels

1. ICY VILLAGE
2. WINK'S HOUSE
3. FOUNTAIN OF ICE
4. SCHOOL
5. LIBRARY
6. SPORTS FIELD
7. BARBERSHOP (WHERE THE WEASELS GET FURCUTS AND CURL THEIR WHISKERS)
8. REALLY COLD LAKE
9. LONFLY WEASEL MANSION
10. ICE-CARVING SHOP

TWO EYES IN THE ICE!

The dragonflies landed the Golden Dragonfly Chariot, and we all got out. Scribblehopper and I explored one little ICE HOUSE after another.

Each building was made completely from ICE, from the WALLS to the FLOOR to the ceiling. But everything inside each house was carved from ice, too! There was ice furniture,

including beds, dressers, tables, and chairs. And each kitchen was full of dishes, glasses, pots, pans, and other knickknacks — all made from ice!

Had the weasels carved all this furniture themselves? And where were the weasels now? Each house was deserted. How strange!

Suddenly, I saw a flash of **movement** in the corner of one ice house.

"Who's there?" I called out.

But there was NO REPLY.

I looked around, but everything in the house was such a BRIGHT WHITE that I couldn't see anything else.

Then I noticed two **shiny black circles** in one corner. What could they be? I approached very slowly.

"Hello?" I said softly. "Is someone there?"

I looked more closely and realized they were two **BRIGHT EYES** shining in the ice!

There was a living **creature** hiding in the corner!

"Who's there?" I asked again. "Don't be scared — we won't **HURT** you!"

A WHITE SHAPE slowly emerged from the corner. The creature held a little paw in front of its brown nose. I stepped forward, and the creature *DASHED* past me and headed toward the door!

I took in the animal's **BLACK-TIPPED** tail and realized it was a weasel! Its fur was so WHITE the creature had been invisible against the ice!

"Wait!" I cried. "Please don't run away. I don't want to **HURT** you — I want to **HELP**!"

"I don't believe you," came a reply. "I don't **trust** you!"

"I come in peace!" I squeaked. "I am Sir Geronimo of Stilton, and I am traveling on behalf of Blossom, Queen of the Fairies!"

The weasel peeked out from behind some ice furniture.

"Are you really the brave and courageous knight?" he asked. "Let me see the ring with *Blossom's crest*! After all that's happened, I don't trust **ANYTHING** or **anyone**!"

I quickly pulled out the ring and showed it to him.

"It looks **real**," the weasel muttered, but he didn't look entirely convinced.

I placed my paw over my **heart**.

"I promise you it's authentic," I said. **"RODENT'S HONOR!"**

Only then did he come toward me, with his paw outstretched.

"My name is **WINK**," he said. "If you'll listen, I'll tell you the sad story of the Blue Weasels . . ."

WINK
THE LAST BLUE WEASEL

The Sad Story of the Blue Weasels

It was a peaceful day, and everything in our village seemed calm. Then the sky suddenly filled with gray clouds, and we smelled a strange odor. A moment later, a flying black ship appeared. A huge net came down from the boat, trapping all my friends! I was the only one who was able to escape, because I am the fastest of the Blue Weasels. (I always win the track races!) I ran to the edge of the village and hid. When I finally returned, I found every house deserted. All of my friends had disappeared!

When Wink had finished telling his tale, Scribblehopper stepped forward.

"I'm Scribblehopper," he told the weasel. "I'm traveling with the knight. I must say, this is very, very **bad**! The knight was supposed to **PROTECT** the Blue Weasels, but he **failed** again!"

He shook his head and looked at me disapprovingly.

"I wouldn't want to be in your **armor** when it's time to tell Queen Blossom what happened to the Blue Weasels, Knight!" He scolded me.

I sighed.

Scribblehopper was right!

I HAD FAILED TO STOP CAPTAIN SHORTTAIL AND HIS PIRATES ONCE AGAIN!

The Blue Weasels

King Weasley and Queen Weasella
The brave leaders of the Blue Weasels

Princess Willow and Prince Winslow
The king and queen's playful twin children

Warbler and Wren
The village's most talented singers

Chef Wendall
The village cook

Wendy
The village messenger

Wilson
The village scholar

Wisefur
The king's advisor

Wilma
Owner of the shop
the Wise Weasel

Winnie
The village seamstress

Wes
The village furstylist

Wendell
The village doctor

Wyatt
The village poet

Wally
The village joker

Wade and Whitney
The village's most spirited
and popular weasels

ONE FOR ALL, AND ALL FOR ONE!

Wink hung his head sadly.

"Now I'm the **L A S T** Blue Weasel left!" he continued. "My friends were probably captured because of their beautiful fur. I get so upset when I think about how **WONDERFUL** our village was before everyone disappeared! Every house was bustling and happy. Oh, I'm so sad and **lonely** now! If only I could find the other Blue Weasels and bring them home. **But how?**"

Scribblehopper wrung his webbed hands, then took out his little chalkboard with the list of treasures we were trying to protect and made an **X** next to "Blue Weasels."

"Our mission was to protect you and your friends," he croaked. "And we failed!

Our village was full of life!

WHAT A SHAME!

"Please stop!" I told the frog. "We can't look **BACK** — we have to move **forward**!"

The dragonflies nodded in agreement, patting me on the back **encouragingly**.

"The knight is right!" they said. Then they **SANG** this song:

"There's only one thing we can do,
Follow Captain Shorttail and his crew!
They stole all the treasures away,
They'll take them to the wizard today!
So it's time for us to roam,
To the scary wizard's home!"

"I'll come with you!" Wink cried. "I would do **anything** to save my friends. And I'm very **FAST**, so I can help with your mission!"

He **scurried** around his house, gathering

I'll come with you!

things for the journey ahead. He pulled on a **blue wool** hat with warm earflaps. Then he pulled a **blue wool** cape over his shoulders. The hem was crusted with **glittering** crystals! Finally, Wink slung a white messenger bag over his arm.

"Okay, I'm **ready** to go!" he said confidently. "One for all, and all for one!"

"One for all, and all for one," Scribblehopper, the dragonflies, and I replied.

"We go in the name of Queen Blossom, the Keeper of Peace and Happiness," I added.

"And we travel in the name of everything in the Kingdom of Fantasy that is **beautiful** and **good**!" Scribblehopper croaked. "We're not **SCARED** of anything! Right, brave Knight?"

"Um, right!" I squeaked, trying my best to

sound **COURAGEOUS**.

And that's how our group of travelers struck out on our ***next adventure***.

We were a strange crew:

A scaredy-mouse ...
A chatty frog ...
A sad, lonely weasel ...
And seven Dragonfly
Princesses!

Even though we were all very different, our hearts were united. We all wanted the same thing: to help Queen Blossom and to save the Kingdom of Fantasy!

The Land of the Whopping Wizard

THE SOUND OF
HEAVY FOOTSTEPS

We climbed into the Golden Dragonfly Chariot,
and the dragonflies beat their wings in unison,
carrying us into the **LAND OF THE
WHOPPING WIZARD**.

"Wow, everything here is really **HUGE**!"
I squeaked as I surveyed the ground below.

"Of course it's **HUGE**!" Scribblehopper
croaked.

A gigantic wall loomed on the horizon.

"B-but that's the **tallest wall** I've ever
seen!" I stuttered fearfully.

"Of course it's tall, Knight," Scribblehopper
replied as he checked our route on his map. "It's
the **Tall Wall of the Whopping Wizard**!"

A castle of staggering size lay beyond the wall.

"Th-that castle is **GIGANTIC**!" I gasped.

Scribblehopper turned to me, exasperated.

"Of course it's **gigantic**, Knight," he shouted, rolling his eyes. "It's the Whopping Wizard's COLOSSAL CASTLE!"

We landed near the Colossal Castle. Suddenly, the earth around us began to **tremble** and **shake** violently. We heard the sound of **VERY HEAVY** footsteps.

"Oh, Knight!" Scribblehopper shrieked in alarm. "Those are the Whopping Wizard's FEARSOME FOOTSTEPS!"

He motioned for us to follow him. Then he ducked behind some GIANT bushes.

"Hurry!" he croaked. *"Let's hide!* Otherwise we'll be squashed by the Whopping Wizard's colossal feet!"

By now, darkness had fallen. We saw the light of a huge torch coming toward us.

The Land of the Whopping Wizard

1. THE TALL WALL
2. THE GIANT DOOR
3. STREET OF FEAR
4. CURVE OF FRIGHT
5. MEGA TREES

6. COLOSSAL CASTLE
7. BIG BRIDGE
8. JUMBO FOUNTAIN
9. GARGANTUAN GARDEN
10. GIGANTIC GREENHOUSE

4

3

ress of Fear   Crystal Castle   Shadow Tower   Darkcastle   Colossal Castle

The torch was as big as an oak tree!

The torch lit a **MONSTROUSLY** large creature:

His face was as big as a castle!

The Whopping Wizard was as tall as a thirteen-story tower. He had eyes as big as **WINDOWS**, a mouth as big as a **DOOR**, and teeth as big as **SHIELDS**.

Holey cheese, he was truly a whopping size!

Holey cheese! He's gigantic!

COLOSSAL FEAR IN THE COLOSSAL CASTLE!

The Whopping Wizard began to sniff the air.

"I smell the odor of mice, frogs, dragonflies, and weasels!" he **BOOMED**.

We trembled with **FEAR** as he held his giant torch up and searched for us in the trees. We ducked behind some bushes, but — alas! A moment later, he found us!

I thought I was about to lose my fur! But instead of **SQUASHING** us under his fearsome feet, the Whopping Wizard plucked us up with his **ENORMOUSE FINGERS**. Each finger was as fat as a tree trunk!

Holey cheese! How terrifying!

He carried us in one hand as he **stomped** toward his Colossal Castle.

Once we were inside that **frightening** castle, the Whopping Wizard headed to the kitchen and placed us on a **HUGE** plate. "**Mmmm!**" he murmured. "I'll eat you all **RAW**, as an appetizer before dinner. **Yum!**"

He seasoned us with giant **salt and pepper shakers**. We all began to sneeze.

Then he poured some **olive oil** on us.

ACHOO! ACHOO! ACHOO!

"I prefer olive oil to butter," he mused.

Then he tossed us into a **COLOSSAL SALAD BOWL**.

Oh no!

It's so slimy!

I'm drowning in oil!

"There!" he said, satisfied. "You're ready to eat! Now I'll go check on my **TREASURES** while I wait for my tea to **cool**."

With that, he **left** the room.

The Dragonfly Princesses tried to fly, but it was impossible because their wings were **soaked in oil**!

So we climbed up the **large spoon** the wizard had left in the bowl.

After a long struggle, we were able to get out. We quickly **BATHED** ourselves in the cup of chamomile tea to wash off the oil. Then we raced toward the door and **squeezed** under it!

Whopping Snores!

On the other side of the door, we found ourselves in an **ENORMOUSE** room with an extremely high ceiling. It was very, very **DARK**.

It was the Whopping Wizard's bedroom!

In the corner was a **COLOSSAL** four-poster bed. The Whopping Wizard was lying there, snoring loudly. He must have decided to take a quick **NAP** before dinner!

ZZZZZZZ . . . ZZZZZZZ . . .

We looked around the room and saw something in the corner near the gigantic window. It sparkled and SHINED in the light of the moon.

It was a **gold throne!**  The wizard had built it using the *treasure of the Golden Gnomes!*

A **colossal crown** encrusted with the EGG OF FIRE was sitting on the throne! It was perched on an oversized, overstuffed velvet cushion.

And an ***immense*** wire net full of snoring Blue Weasels was right next to the throne!

Finally, the *silver coffer* was on the floor right in front of the gigantic golden chair. I tiptoed over and peeked inside . . .

It was full of a **sweet-smelling** gold powder. It was the Vanilla Fairies'

famouse **magic vanilla dust**!

"Psst! Knight!" the dragonflies whispered. "What do we do **NOW**?"

"We need a plan!" Scribblehopper croaked. "Come on, Knight! *Let's go!* Come up with a plan, a plan, a plan!"

He snapped his fingers at me: Snap! Snap! Snap!

I tried to **THINK**, but Scribblehopper's snapping was so distracting!

"Please, be quiet!" I whispered. "I need to CONCENTRATE to come up with a plan!"

I looked around the room, trying to think of something.

The stolen objects were all very **LARGE** and **heavy**. If we tried to move something, it would be **NoiSY**. We might wake the Whopping Wizard!

I looked from the **throne** to the **crown** to the **weasels** to the *silver coffer* full of **VaNiLLa DuSt**. Hmmm. The **VaNiLLa DuSt** . . .

I brightened as a brilliant idea came to me. We could use a **pinch** of vanilla dust to make the throne, the crown, the net full of weasels, and the silver coffer all **float** quietly into the air and **out the window**! Then we could transport the objects through the Kingdom of Fantasy and back to Queen Blossom!

My friends really liked my **plan**.

Here's what we'll do . . .

Mmmm, it smells good!

1. Scribblehopper, Wink, and I will sprinkle a little vanilla dust on our heads.

Look at me!

2. Then we'll be able to fly!

3. We'll sprinkle some dust on the objects we want to transport . . .

4. And the objects will float out the window!

A MASSIVE SURPRISE!

We used the Whopping Wizard's belt to tie all the **magical objects** together. Then we opened the gigantic window and **FLOATED** out of the castle, pulling the stolen treasures along behind us.

Scribblehopper, Wink, and I

the vanilla dust
made everything float
out the window!

floated in the air next to the flying dragonflies. We waved our arms as if they were wings, flying **HIGHER** and **HIGHER**.

Suddenly, there was a loud **CLUNK**!

The throne had **SLAMMED** into the edge of the window, waking the Whopping Wizard.

Colossal cannonballs! **"COLOSSAL CANNONBALLS!"** he shouted. "They're getting away with my **precious treasures**!"

He dashed out of the **COLOSSAL CASTLE** and ran after us. But his huge feet tripped over some huge trees, and he fell down with a **COLOSSAL CRASH**! He began to

roll down a massive hill. But as he rolled, something amazing happened: He began to **fall apart**!

First his **foot** fell off, then an **ARM**, and a **shoulder**. There were **wheels** and **gears** and **screws** and **BOLTS** and **pistons** everywhere! The Whopping Wizard was really a giant robot!

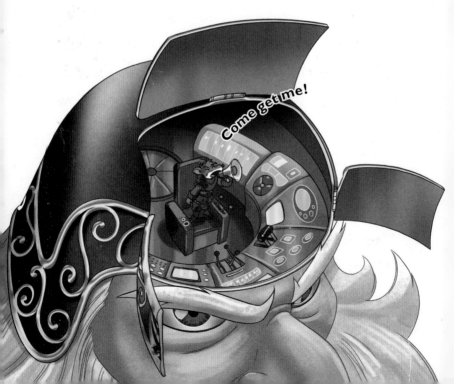

But who was controlling the colossal robot?

THE ANSWER WAS A MASSIVE SURPRISE!

As the wizard tumbled down the hill, a minuscule door in the wizard's giant head POPPED open. Inside was a tiny mouse squeaking THREATENINGLY into a megaphone:

"This isn't the end, you little pests!

I'll be back, oh yes! I'll make you pay for stealing my treasures! If it weren't for you all, I would still be the WHOPPING WIZARD. Now I've lost everything. What's worse, now everyone knows I'm not a great and powerful wizard but a tiny mouse! But don't worry, I'll get my REVENGE, or my name isn't SPITFIRE THE PIRATE!"

Then he turned toward the sky.

"Captain Shorttail and the **Pirates of the Ship of Secrets**!" he shouted into his

megaphone. "Come rescue me, you fools!"

A moment later we smelled the disgusting stench of **rotten algae** and filthy fish bones as the **Ship of Secrets** appeared above us in the sky.

Captain Shorttail and his crew used their **ANCHOR** to rescue **Spitfire**. Then they flew off in the opposite direction as we *joined hands* and flew together toward Queen Blossom and the Kingdom of the Fairies!

When we arrived at CRYSTAL CASTLE, the fairies waiting there cheered loudly. What a wonderful happy ending to our **INCREDIBLE ADVENTURE**!

LONG LIVE KING GOLDHEART!

As we hovered over Crystal Castle, I saw *Queen Blossom* and her dear friend Sweet Melinda walking together.

We landed in front of them and placed the treasures we had retrieved at Blossom's feet. The Blue Weasels scrambled out of the net.

"Yay, we're free!" they shouted with gℓ𝒆𝒆.

"Here are the stolen TREASURES, my queen!" I said. "I'm happy to report that the Whopping Wizard is no longer a danger. He wasn't even a *real* wizard! He was a SMALL, surly mouse operating a COLOSSAL robot! He said his name was Spitfire the Pirate. Do you know him?"

Blossom nodded. "Unfortunately, I do," she said. "He may be *small*, but he's **big trouble**!"

Spitfire the Pirate

He is Captain Shorrtail's evil cousin and a top-notch inventor. He constructed the Whopping Wizard robot to scare everyone in the Kingdom of Fantasy and take over as king. Thanks to Geronimo and his friends, Spitfire's evil plan failed!

Then Blossom smiled. She had a big surprise for me!

"Knight, this was your teNth MiSSiON in the Kingdom of Fantasy, and you completed it **successfully**," she said, smiling. "As a reward, I would like to create a new KINGDOM for you. I know you will be an excellent leader because you are *good* and *just*!"

"That might be true, Queen, but you should know about all the mistakes the knight made!" Scribblehopper blurted out.

I turned as red as a **TOMATO**.

"Well, we all make **mistakes**," Blossom replied kindly. "It's how we correct them that matters! Knight, what do you say we call you King Goldheart of the *Kingdom of Generous Hearts*?"

"That would be **wonderful**, Your Majesty!" I squeaked happily. "Thank you!"

Blossom tapped my head with her magic wand. Then she sang sweetly:

"Fairies, sound the magic horn,

For today a new land is born.

A place for creatures good and kind,

Those brave in both heart and mind.

The king's a very worthy knight,

A mouse who's daring, bold, and bright!

Make his crown gold like his name,

King Goldheart, I wish you luck and fame!"

"Hip, hip, hooray!" everyone yelled in unison. "Long live **King Goldheart** of the *Kingdom of Generous Hearts!*"

A fairy handed me a **GOLD RING** carved with the **symbol** of the king! I also received a flag with the *Goldheart family crest* and motto. It read: *Those who give things lovingly give twice as much!*

I was so moved a tear **rolled** down my snout.

"Congratulations, Your Majesty," she said. "You earned this honor for your **courage**: It's thanks to you that my kingdom and I are **SAFE**! You and I will always be friends, and our kingdoms will **FOREVER** be allies."

She and Queen Blossom both smiled at me. I felt **humbled** to receive such a great honor from two **VERY DEAR FRIENDS**!

"Queen Blossom, thank you," I said. "I hope I'll make you proud as king! But what will happen to my kingdom when I am at home in **New Mouse City**? Sooner or later, I must return to my friends and family there!"

Scribblehopper coughed.

"Knight, if you would entrust me with your kingdom, I could be **viceroy**," he said hesitantly. "I will act as **KING** instead of you whenever you can't be there."

"That's a great idea, Scribblehopper!" I replied. "Of course you can be viceroy."

He began to do a little **jig** as he sang this song:

"Hooray, hooray, do a happy dance,
It's time to sing and twirl and prance!
My heart is full of love and joy,
I'm going to be viceroy!
With my friends, I'll celebrate,
This little twist of froggy fate.
Oh, I'm feeling such great bliss,
Sir Knight, let me give you a kiss!"

Scribblehopper leaned forward to place a *smooch* on my snout just as I **kicked up** my paws in a cheerful dance move. I lost my balance and slipped, *TUMBLING* into the fountain behind me.

"Ahhhh!" I yelled. "My crown!"

I fell **down** . . .

and **down** . . .

and **down** through the water.

I'm going to be viceroy!

Ahhhh! My crown!

And then I began floating **up** . . .

and **up** . . .

and **up**!

I was returning home to . . .

Return to
New Mouse City

NO MORE KISSES!

"My crown!" I squeaked. "Give me back MY CROWN!"

I heard a female mouse **giggle**.

"Don't worry, Geronimo," she said. "Here's your crown!"

A second later, someone plunked a crown on my head. I reached up to touch it, but I realized right away that it wasn't the DELICATE GOLD CROWN Queen Blossom had given me in the Kingdom of Fantasy. No, this was the FROG PRINCE'S fake crown, straight from Felicia Fashionfur's costume shop, Masks for Mice. And the voice was coming from my date for the Grand Masked Ball, CREEPELLA VON CACKLEFUR!

"Oh, my frog prince, I like you with or without a crown!" Creepella shouted. Then she reached for my paw and **kissed** it.

"Enough, please!" I squeaked desperately. "No more kisses!"

I jumped to my paws and climbed out of the fountain, still GROGGY. I looked around and realized I really was back in *New Mouse City*.

Oh, my frog prince!

Ha, ha, ha!

Yes, I was at Goldenfur Castle in New Mouse City, and I was surrounded by a crowd of guests at the *Grand Masked Ball*. We were all dressed in costumes — there were fairies, **WITCHES**, knights, **gnomes**, and pixies all around me . . .

But I was no longer in the Kingdom of Fantasy!

Hey, frog prince!

Now I remember . . .

I touched my sore head again, remembering what had happened: **CREEPELLA** swung her purse at me . . .

As I dodged her, I slipped and fell into **Goldenfur Castle's** Water lily Fountain.

And then I hit my head and **fainted**!

I DREAMED that I was in the magical *Kingdom of Fantasy*, where I was the hero in a fabumouse ADVENTURE!

Knight.

It had

all been an

INCREDIBLE

DREAM!

WONDERFUL NEW MOUSE CITY!

I excused myself from the crowd of party guests and went out onto the terrace. There, I BREATHED in the fresh night air under the light of an enormouse **full moon**. I gazed out over my beloved home on **Mouse Island**, taking in the rolling hills, tall buildings, and the sea beyond.

OH, HOW I LOVED THE WONDERFUL NEW MOUSE CITY!

And yet, for a second, I was filled with **nostalgia** as I remembered my many journeys through the **mythical** Kingdom of Fantasy. I couldn't believe this had been my **tenth** adventure! It was one of the **best** ones

yet: I had been given my very own kingdom, where I was **CROWNED** king!

Even if it had been just a **DREAM**, I reminded myself that it's what's in the **Heart** that counts. And in my **Heart**, I always enjoy helping Queen Blossom and all of the **fascinating** creatures I meet in the Kingdom of Fantasy! I figured I might as well **ENJOY** the moment. Who knew if I would ever return to that **WONDERFUL** place again? Who knew if the **Kingdom of Generous Hearts** was there awaiting my return? Who knew if Scribblehopper was doing his **JOB** as King Goldheart's viceroy?

A TEAR RAN DOWN MY SNOUT.

Maybe my friends in the Kingdom of Fantasy had already *forgotten* me! Well, even if they had, I would NEVER forget them. Every memory, every feeling, and every emotion I had experienced in the Kingdom of Fantasy would forever be IMPRINTED ON MY HEART! I would never forget anything about my incredible adventure.

I hope you enjoyed dreaming along with me!

So good-bye until my next dream,
and my next journey in the
fabumouse Kingdom of Fantasy!
It'll be another whisker-licking-
good adventure,
and that's a promise.

Rodent's honor!

FANTASIAN ALPHABET

A B C D E

F G H I J

K L M N O

P Q R S T

U V W X Y Z

0 1 2 3 4 5 6 7 8 9

ABOUT THE AUTHOR

 Born in New Mouse City, Mouse Island, **GERONIMO STILTON** is Rattus Emeritus of Mousomorphic Literature and of Neo-Ratonic Comparative Philosophy. For the past twenty years, he has been running *The Rodent's Gazette*, New Mouse City's most widely read daily newspaper.

Stilton was awarded the Ratitzer Prize for his scoops on *The Curse of the Cheese Pyramid* and *The Search for Sunken Treasure*. He has also received the Andersen 2000 Prize for Personality of the Year. One of his bestsellers won the 2002 eBook Award for world's best ratlings' electronic book. His works have been published all over the globe.

In his spare time, Mr. Stilton collects antique cheese rinds and plays golf. But what he most enjoys is telling stories to his nephew Benjamin.

Don't miss any of my adventures in the Kingdom of Fantasy!

THE KINGDOM OF FANTASY

THE QUEST FOR PARADISE:
THE RETURN TO THE KINGDOM OF FANTASY

THE AMAZING VOYAGE:
THE THIRD ADVENTURE IN THE KINGDOM OF FANTASY

THE DRAGON PROPHECY:
THE FOURTH ADVENTURE IN THE KINGDOM OF FANTASY

THE VOLCANO OF FIRE:
THE FIFTH ADVENTURE IN THE KINGDOM OF FANTASY

THE SEARCH FOR TREASURE:
THE SIXTH ADVENTURE IN THE KINGDOM OF FANTASY

THE ENCHANTED CHARMS:
THE SEVENTH ADVENTURE IN THE KINGDOM OF FANTASY

THE PHOENIX OF DESTINY:
AN EPIC KINGDOM OF FANTASY ADVENTURE

THE HOUR OF MAGIC:
THE EIGHTH ADVENTURE IN THE KINGDOM OF FANTASY

THE WIZARD'S WAND:
THE NINTH ADVENTURE IN THE KINGDOM OF FANTASY

THE SHIP OF SECRETS:
THE TENTH ADVENTURE IN THE KINGDOM OF FANTASY

THE DRAGON OF FORTUNE:
AN EPIC KINGDOM OF FANTASY ADVENTURE

Be sure to read all my fabumouse adventures!

#1 Lost Treasure of the Emerald Eye

#2 The Curse of the Cheese Pyramid

#3 Cat and Mouse in a Haunted House

#4 I'm Too Fond of My Fur!

#5 Four Mice Deep in the Jungle

#6 Paws Off, Cheddarface!

#7 Red Pizzas for a Blue Count

#8 Attack of the Bandit Cats

#9 A Fabumouse Vacation for Geronimo

#10 All Because of a Cup of Coffee

#11 It's Halloween, You 'Fraidy Mouse!

#12 Merry Christmas, Geronimo!

#13 The Phantom of the Subway

#14 The Temple of the Ruby of Fire

#15 The Mona Mousa Code

#16 A Cheese-Colored Camper

#17 Watch Your Whiskers, Stilton!

#18 Shipwreck on the Pirate Islands

#19 My Name Is Stilton, Geronimo Stilton

#20 Surf's Up, Geronimo!

#21 The Wild, Wild West

#22 The Secret of Cacklefur Castle

A Christmas Tale

#23 Valentine's Day
Disaster

#24 Field Trip to
Niagara Falls

#25 The Search for
Sunken Treasure

#26 The Mummy
with No Name

#27 The Christmas
Toy Factory

#28 Wedding
Crasher

#29 Down and Out
Down Under

#30 The Mouse Island
Marathon

#31 The Mysterious
Cheese Thief

Christmas Catastrophe

#32 Valley of the
Giant Skeletons

#33 Geronimo and the
Gold Medal Mystery

#34 Geronimo Stilton,
Secret Agent

#35 A Very Merry
Christmas

#36 Geronimo's
Valentine

#37 The Race Across
America

#38 A Fabumouse
School Adventure

#39 Singing Sensation

#40 The Karate Mouse

#41 Mighty Mount
Kilimanjaro

#42 The Peculiar
Pumpkin Thief

#43 I'm Not a
Supermouse!

#44 The Giant
Diamond Robbery

#45 Save the White
Whale!

#46 The Haunted
Castle

#47 Run for the Hills, Geronimo!

#48 The Mystery in Venice

#49 The Way of the Samurai

#50 This Hotel Is Haunted!

#51 The Enormouse Pearl Heist

#52 Mouse in Space!

#53 Rumble in the Jungle

#54 Get into Gear, Stilton!

#55 The Golden Statue Plot

#56 Flight of the Red Bandit

The Hunt for the Golden Book

#57 The Stinky Cheese Vacation

#58 The Super Chef Contest

#59 Welcome to Moldy Manor

The Hunt for the Curious Cheese

#60 The Treasure of Easter Island

#61 Mouse House Hunter

#62 Mouse Overboard!

The Hunt for the Secret Papyrus

#63 The Cheese Experiment

#64 Magical Mission

#65 Bollywood Burglary

The Hunt for the Hundredth Key

#66 Operation: Secret Recipe

#67 The Chocolate Chase